# Tales
# of the
# Suburbs

# Biography

JUSTIN DAVID is a child of Wolverhampton who has lived and worked in East London for most of his adult life. He graduated from the MA Creative and Life Writing at Goldsmiths, University of London and is a founder member of Leather Lane Writers. His debut novella, *The Pharmacist*, was described in the Times Literary Supplement as '*the perfect introduction to a singular voice in gay literature*.' *Tales of the Suburbs* is the first book in the Welston World Sagas.

He is also a well-known photographer. His images of artists, writers, performers and musicians have appeared on the pages of numerous publications including—The Times, The Guardian, Attitude, Beige, Gay Times, QX and Time Out.

Justin is one half of Inkandescent with Nathan Evans. Their first offering, *Threads*, featuring Nathan's poetry and Justin's photography, was long-listed for the Polari First Book Prize. It was supported using public funding by Arts Council England. In 2021, amidst the Covid-19 pandemic, they published their first collection, ~~MAIN~~STREAM: *An Anthology of Stories from the Edges,* championing underrepresented voices. They also published *Address Book* by Neil Bartlett, an Observer Book of the Year, which has since been shortlisted for the Polari Prize.

Praise for Justin David and
*Tales of the Suburbs*

'Justin David's Tales of the Suburbs reveals a true writer's gift for comic and poignant storytelling, in which pithy dialogue and sharp characterisation make for compelling reading.'
PATRICIA ROUTLEDGE

'A well-observed, charming account of small-town, working-class life and the move to the big, bad, brilliant city. This should strike a chord not just with gay readers but with anyone who's lived, loved and fought to become the person they're meant to be.'
MATT CAIN

'Justin David's tale of working-class gay life is a bitter-sweet, beautiful thing. The audience at Polari loved it—as well they should.'
PAUL BURSTON, Polari Literary Salon

Praise for Justin David and
*Kissing the Lizard*

'This beautifully creepy novella manages to be both macabre and terrifying, yet also shot through with a humour that is blacker than black. I loved it and devoured it in one sitting.'
SJ WATSON, author of *Before I Go to Sleep*

'*Kissing the Lizard* is a study of insidious enticement that gathers into a contemporary nightmare, all the more frightening for its quietness, and the prose is as vital as the colourful cast of characters.'
RAMSEY CAMPBELL

'There's not much rarer than a working class voice in fiction, except maybe a gay working class voice. We need writers like Justin David.'
PAUL McVEIGH, author of *The Good Son*

Praise for Justin David and
*The Pharmacist*

'As lubricious as early Alan Hollinghurst, *The Pharmacist* is a welcome
reissue from Inkandescent, and the perfect introduction to a singular voice
in gay literature.'
JUDE COOK, THE TIMES LITERARY SUPPLEMENT

'*The Pharmacist* is a rare thing of perfection: a contemporary novella that
reads like both a European classic and a page-turner. The writing is superb.
Sense of place, story, insight into the human condition, gave me everything
that I wanted from a work of fiction. Not five stars but an entire galaxy!'
VG LEE, author of *Mr Oliver's Object of Desire*

'At the heart of David's *The Pharmacist* is an oddly touching and bizarre love
story, a modern day Harold and Maude set in the drugged-up world of
pre-gentrification Shoreditch. The dialogue, especially, bristles with glorious
life.'
JONATHAN KEMP, author of *London Triptych*

'A drug-fuelled, drug-fucked, sweat and semen-drenched exploration
of love and loss in the deathly hallows of twenty-first century London.
Justin David's prose is as sharp as a hypodermic needle. Unflinching,
uncomfortable but always compelling, *The Pharmacist* finds the true meaning
of love in the most unlikely places.'
NEIL McKENNA, author of *Fanny and Stella*

'Sexy, wistful, wise, haunting and totally full of surprises. A real ride.'
NINA WADIA

# Tales of the Suburbs

Part One of the Welston World Sagas

## Justin David

Inkandescent

by outsiders for outsiders

## Inkandescent

First published by Inkandescent, 2023
Text Copyright © 2023 Justin David
Cover Design Copyright © 2023 Joe Mateo

Publisher's note: a version of *Tales of the Suburbs* was included within
*He's Done Ever So Well for Himself* by Justin David,
published by Inkandescent in 2018

A CIP catalogue record for this book
is available from the British Library

Printed in the UK by Severn, Gloucester

ISBN 978-1-912620-24-1 (paperback)
ISBN 978-1-912620-25-8 (ebook)

1 3 5 7 9 10 8 6 4 2

www.inkandescent.co.uk

For my Uncle Keith
*nothing but a bloody varmint*

# Contents

*'And children who need to be able to count and multiply are learning anti-racist mathematics—whatever that may be. Children who need to be able to express themselves in clear English are being taught political slogans. Children who need to be taught to respect traditional moral values are being taught that they have an inalienable right to be gay. And children who need encouragement—and children do so much need encouragement—so many children—they are being taught that our society offers them no future. All of those children are being cheated of a sound start in life—yes, cheated.'*

*Speech to Tory Party Conference, 1987*
MARGARET THATCHER 1925—2013

# Unicorn

*Flamboyant.* There's a word. Jamie's thinking about popstars when he notices the bright red wool starting to unravel. 'I've dropped a stitch,' he tells Nan.

'Don't pull it, love. Give it here,' she says. She fixes it with her usual confidence. Just like that. Jamie loves being with Nan. She runs her papery fingers over the length of knitting beginning to form under the last row of stitches. 'Clever boy, ain't ya, our Jamie.' He can hear her voice but his eyes are fixed on the scrapbook in his lap, bulging with cuttings—photographs of popstars he's collected. Jamie takes Nan's ballpoint pen from the arm of the chair and writes the word *flamboyant* at the bottom of a list he's started. 'Tension's a bit wobbly,' she points out. 'Nice and neat though—try to keep the wool taut when you bring it round the needle.' She finishes the row for him. 'There. That row was knit. Next row, purl.' She looks out of the window and nudges him. 'Look how dark it is a'ready. Not even five o'clock yet.'

Gazing into the tangerine twilight beyond the net curtains, Jamie's eyes become unfocused. His head fills with boys in turbans, quiffs and sequins, singers in eye-patches, feather boas and hairspray. This world of dry ice and neon and starburst light is only usually glimpsed in between the news and *Tomorrow's World* on Thursday nights and he wonders what happens to it when Grandad switches channels. While he likes to float off into his dream world, Nan has her own special way of keeping him in this one. 'That cabbage'll be done soon.'

It's quiet bar the bubbling pot in the kitchen and the ticking of the clock on the mantelpiece. Jamie puts the knitting down and sips the orange cordial mixed with a bit of whiskey that she allows him every Saturday evening— just him and Nan having special time. *Special time* means everything else stops. Television and radio off, Nan and Jamie do something together—sometimes bake a cake, sometimes crochet.

He lets his eyes pass over everything he loves in the room—Nan's Tretchikoff: a girl with red lips and a blue face hanging against embossed wallpaper, the cabinet of collected snow-globes, three carved wooden African figurines—until his eyes reach Grandad slouched in his armchair. His face is mottled with dark patches of skin and his eyes are red and wet, making him look both sad and angry at the same time. He used to be different. He used to be distinguished and sort of proud. Always had time to teach Jamie new things. They made a bird-scarer for the allotment and spent ages doing giant jigsaws. They loved spending time together. But all that has stopped. Poor Grandad.

Next to him is a pile of unread large-print library books covered with sticky backed plastic. There's also a scattering of rags, which he uses to wipe his runny nose, *festered*, Jamie's mum would say, from too much booze. He's joining parts of a model Spitfire together with a little tube of glue, which he's been doing since he lost his job as an electrician at the washing machine factory. Now he mumbles things under his breath: 'Boys of his age should be out chasing wenches, not messing around with wool. When I was his age... I used to have 'em flocking.'

'Oh, yes Alf,' Nan will nod. 'Heard it all before. Proper bloody Casanova.' This has been happening a lot recently; she'll say something cruel just to shut him up. The other day he'd been moaning about his waterworks playing up and she told him that if he didn't stop dribbling on the bathroom carpet, she would 'cut it off' while he was asleep.

Jamie's mum says it's difficult for Grandad to find a new job, him being too old to retrain and younger men prepared to work for less money. These men know about computers and stuff, which Grandad does not. His mum says Grandad is depressed. Jamie hasn't a clue what that means.

Grandad puts his glue down and looks at Jamie. Then he looks at the knitting, with an unhappy, disapproving sneer, shakes his head and turns back to his model without saying a word. Why is he being like this? Jamie tries not to dwell on it. The clock shows five o'clock and his head is filling with popstars again, like the ones in his scrapbook: frilly shirts, lipstick, boys wearing eyeliner, dandy highwaymen, crazy female singers in white lacy dresses.

A car pulls up outside. There's the rev of an engine, doors slamming and then laughter. Nan jumps up out of her seat, runs to the window and lifts the net. 'It's them.' She lets the net drop and points to Grandad's Spitfire. 'Put that up now, Alf. They're here. Come on. There ain't room in here to swing a cat.'

Grandad huffs and puffs and grumbles. He leaves the Spitfire where it is. 'Why does everything have to change when that lot arrive? Bloody nuisance. We do *live* here, you know!' He used to leap up to answer the door when someone knocked, but not these days.

Nan dashes about the room clearing things away, collecting anything enjoyable. She moves the pipe that Grandad has loaded with tobacco but not bothered to smoke and the glass of whiskey he's poured but not bothered to drink and slams them away in his cabinet. She picks up a Curly Wurly from the mantelpiece and stuffs it into her pinny. Arms full, she points at Grandad's bag of pork scratchings until he stuffs them, reluctantly, into his pocket. 'Freddie eats whatever he sees,' she says, heading for the back room clutching the fruit bowl. 'Jamie. Quick!' She points at his knitting. 'Put that up.'

Jamie doesn't need to be told. He's already wrapping the wool around the needles, stuffing them into the tapestry-covered bag that she'd given him to keep all his things inside. As Nan darts back in from the kitchen and over to the window, the smell of cabbage wafts in after her. *Must be boiled to nothing now*, Jamie thinks. Then he's startled by the thump of a knuckle against the window and a face pressed against the glass.

'Oh, look at ya!' Nan moans at Auntie Sandra's face through the curtain. 'Get yer nose off the glass, varmint! I've only just cleaned them windows.' Nan goes into the hallway and cheers as Auntie Sandra appears. Behind her is a deeper, louder voice: 'Hello Phyllis. Where's Nancy Boy?' Uncle Freddie sticks his head in sideways round the doorframe and grins—resting his black moustache on the edge of the door. Then his whole body appears, pushed in by Nan.

'Get in there—pest!' she says. That's her way of saying she loves Freddie—*pest, varmint*, and a good whack around the ears. They all like him. But Jamie doesn't get to see him very often as he's always on the beat. Nan's glasses are still steamed up. She wipes them on her pinny. 'He's here again, ain't he, upsetting the applecart. Just don't bloody eat anything. You hear? Or I'll have your guts f'garters.'

Freddie looks past her at Jamie. '*There* you are, Nancy Boy,' he says. It makes Jamie cringe, that name. Uncle Freddie says it's a term of endearment, but deep down, Jamie knows Freddie is being mean. He throws himself on the floor with his scrapbook.

On TV is some quiz show that Nan and Grandad like to watch, with a toy bin as a booby prize. Jamie turns the pages of popstars: Steve Strange, Midge Ure, Toyah Wilcox, Kate Bush. Behind him, he can hear a right commotion, Nan and Auntie Sandra laughing together.

'Alright Pops?' Uncle Freddie says, enthusiastically trying to fetch some life out of Grandad and failing miserably.

'Allo Dad,' Auntie Sandra says.

Grandad just mumbles, eyes super-glued to the television screen.

Jamie turns onto his back and rests on his elbows just in time to see Auntie Sandra staring at Nan, as if there is something she wants to say about Grandad. Nan is sneering at him. Looking back at Sandra, she shakes her head. There's a look of concern and confusion on Auntie Sandra's face, but it disappears when she notices Jamie looking at her.

'Alright our Jamie?' She smiles one of her big sunbeams that make him feel like the most important person in the world. He doesn't get to see her very often either because she's training to become a schoolteacher. 'You been keeping Nan and Grandad company?'

'Been making a pencil case.' Jamie points at the tapestry covered knitting bag with his things stuffed inside.

'Oh have you? You can knit me a mohair cardi next.' Her voice is full of belief. She always says Jamie can do anything if he puts his mind to it.

'Made anything else?' Uncle Freddie asks, prodding him on the shoulder.

Nan tugs the collar of Freddie's denim jacket. 'Ain't you come to stay?' she asks and goes into the kitchen. 'I'll put the kettle on,' she calls.

Uncle Freddie throws his jacket off, revealing a white t-shirt with the words FRANKIE SAYS RELAX printed in bold, black letters across the chest. Everyone's wearing them. He thinks he's really cool. He perches himself on the arm of the settee, folds his arms and sits looking at Jamie, as if he knows a secret. Auntie Sandra gets down on her knees next to Jamie. Her golden frizz of curls dangles in his face. It's lovely when they are all together. There's always a lot of talk and laughter, but recently less from Grandad. Now he just grumbles about *privatisation* and *trade unions* and other things Jamie doesn't understand.

'Oi. Nance,' Uncle Freddie calls to him. 'Have you done it?'

'Done what?' Sandra asks, not appreciating being kept out of the secret.

'*He* knows!' Uncle Freddie nods.

Auntie Sandra slaps Freddie's leg. 'Leave him alone *you!*' She turns back to him. She smells of hairspray. 'Aintcha gonna give me a kiss?'

Jamie kisses her. Then she reaches into the pocket of her stonewashed denim jacket and pulls out a piece of paper. 'I found this stuffed in between the pages of my diary. It's an old one but I thought you'd like it for your scrapbook.'

Jamie knows what it is without even looking. She always saves them for him—clippings from her *Look-In* magazines—lots of them. Pictures of famous popstars

23

photographed in nightclubs, or stills from pop videos. He takes the clipping in his hands and slowly unfolds it, taking care not to tear it, as if it's a special Christmas present.

'Wow.' It's Boy George and his friend Marilyn. George has a geisha white face, heavily shaded eyes, glitter on the lips, and his famous braids. Marilyn is doing her trademark look: bright red lips against a powder white face and sharp cheekbones. She's smiling brightly. All teeth. *Glamour*.

When Nan comes back into the room, Uncle Freddie is eating a Curly Wurly he's found in Grandad's cookie jar, so she cracks him over the head with the back of her hand. 'Bloody gannet!'

'Ow! What was that for?' he says, eyes tearing up.

'I've told you before. Stop eating my bleedin' chocolate!'

'That hurt.'

'It'll hurt even more if I do it again,' she says, arm half-cocked ready to give him another one.

'You caught me with your wedding ring. Gonna have a right lump now.'

Nan cracks him again, even harder this time.

'What was that for?' Uncle Freddie rubs his head.

'That's for next time,' Nan says, looking very satisfied with herself.

Jamie and Sandra giggle and turn back to the photo of Boy George and Marilyn. 'Look at it, Jamie.'

'Amazing, ain't it,' he says.

Sandra spreads the photo flat under her fingers and smooths out the creases. 'Imagine doing your shopping and seeing that.' She strokes the image of Boy George with a painted fingertip. 'So much... what's the word? *Mystique.*'

'D'you think you'd ever see Boy George on the street? I mean in London. Would you see him out?'

'Course,' she says. 'Pop stars *must* leave their homes— just like everyone else.'

Jamie shakes his head. 'He'd have servants,' he says. '*And* a driver. *And* someone to do his make-up.' They have this conversation a lot, Sandra and Jamie. They know that you'd be very lucky to see a pop star with your own eyes, but they both agree even pop stars have to go shopping, so if you tried really hard, you might find one being chased by a crowd of photographers.

Sandra tilts her head and says, 'I think I'd wet myself if I saw him and Marilyn knocking about the town, shopping for clothes.'

Jamie looks at the image of Marilyn—such a beautiful girl. Somehow, he knows she is much more than that. More beautiful than any girl he's seen before. *Dazzling.* Beyond human. 'Sandra, is Marilyn his girlfriend?'

'No, Jamie. I don't think she's his *girlfriend.* I think they're mates.' She winks at him and then taps the picture again. 'If you saw that in the street, it'd be like seeing a mythological creature.'

*Mythological?* Now there's a word. They'd done myths and legends at school. 'You mean like something from a fairy tale?'

'Yeah.'

Was Boy George a boy? Or was he a girl with a boy's name? Jamie wonders if anyone in his family really knows what he is. No one has ever seen anything like him. Nevertheless, they all love Boy George's music when it comes on the wireless.

Jamie grabs the sellotape from the mantelpiece and tapes the picture into his scrapbook. At the bottom of his list of words he writes *mythological*. Under the image of Boy George, he writes another word—*Unicorn*—and shows it to Sandra. She smiles. Perhaps he can use that word in a story he'll write later.

Uncle Freddie pipes up. 'So, Nancy Boy, have you done it?'

Jamie decides that if Freddie calls him that name once more he'll kick him really hard in the shins. He hates being teased by him and he isn't going to take it anymore.

When he turns over onto his back, Freddie is flexing his biceps.

'I've done it, alright.' Jamie blows out a loud sigh.

Nan is warming the backs of her legs near the fire. 'Oh, Freddie, just wait till you see it. He's made such a good job of it. Come on Jamie. Time for the unveiling.' She claps.

'Unveiling of what?' Sandra asks.

'Go and get it then,' Uncle Freddie says, impatiently.

'Who's Auntie Sandra going as?'

'Is this about the fancy-dress party?' Sandra makes an excited squeal.

'Kate Bush,' Uncle Freddie replies.

'Uncle Freddie, are you going to wear the makeup as well?'

Nan tuts. 'He's not your real uncle yet. They're not married.' She shoots Grandad a stare.

'Course I'm going to wear make-up,' Uncle Freddie continues. 'Only for this though.'

Jamie sits upright. 'Sandra, d'you think Boy George looks like that *all* the time?'

Sandra giggles. 'I read that he doesn't leave the house without a full face of slap.'

Jamie tries to imagine the world that he comes from—a strange place where people don't have to be boys *or* girls. They can be a mix. And nobody cares. But the boys who don't behave enough like boys at school either get beaten up or ignored. That's how it is. Except in the pages of his scrapbook—not one of them looks like any of the boys and girls he knows from school.

'Funny looking thing, ain't he?' Nan says, tilting her head to look at Boy George. Nan can't really get a grip on him. To her, popstars look like Buddy Holly. Or Cliff Richard, perhaps?

'Not right, if you ask me,' Grandad says, tapping a finger

on the side of his head.

Nan plants her hands on her hips. 'Nobody asked *you*,' she says.

'Bloody whoopsies,' Grandad says. 'I blame Thatcher.'

'Oh yes… Thatcher's to blame for everything, isn't she?' Nan says. 'She'll be to blame for why I'm still waiting for a new fridge freezer, or why the windows are never cleaned, or why I always have to change a plug around this place, or why you can't afford your own daughter's wedding dr—' Her tear-filled eyes snap onto Sandra who by now has completely lost her smile.

*Oh no.* They're not going to start all this again. Jamie's never seen her quite like this. She raises a trembling finger. 'Sandra! I swear if something doesn't change soon, I'll get the carving knife to him. I will.'

Jamie knows he shouldn't interrupt but he can't help himself. 'Nan, what's a *whoopsie?*'

'Oh dear God!' Nan rolls her eyes. 'Live and let live. That's my motto.' She looks at his scrapbook. 'There's enough heartache in the world. A man in make-up ain't hurting no one.'

Now seems like the perfect moment to go upstairs and get the creation he's made for Uncle Freddie.

Nan's bedroom is goldfish orange. The walls are orange, the bedspread is orange, even the carpet is orange. He likes Nan's bedroom. It's cosy and happy and full of pretty things that she's collected, like giant spiky seashells and seahorses she's trapped in little blocks of resin and made into paperweights and fancy fabric lampshades with furry tassels. Nan's very fond of cacti and has five different types lined up on the windowsill, which Jamie often dares himself to stroke. One day one of the spikes got stuck in his finger and he screamed blue murder until Nan picked it out between her false teeth.

The orange curtains are open but it's dark outside so he goes over to draw them. It's so dark he can see a trillion pinpoints of streetlight in pebbles of rainwater that have formed on the glass like the skin of a tangerine. He can just make out the row of houses opposite with their borders of privet and cars parked outside. Over the rooftops he can see the streetlights getting smaller as they stretch away into the distance until the last thing he can see is the floodlight of the factory where Grandad works. *Used* to work. He's been 'laid off'.

When Jamie was really little, his friend Stephen told him those lights were at the end of the world and Jamie was daft enough to believe him. Now, of course, he knows that it isn't true because Boy George is from London. You can't see London because it's hundreds of miles away, but the lights of Grandad's factory, well they are only in the next town.

Jamie closes the curtains and turns to Nan's dressing table where his favourite photograph of young Nan and young Grandad stands in a gilt frame. You can tell it's really old because it's in black and white. Jamie used to think that everything in the world was grey in the olden days, just like in the pictures. In the photograph Nan's hair is black and done all nice in curls like an actress. Grandad looks young and macho like a real man from a Hollywood movie. This is how he likes to think of them. Some artist has gone over the picture with a pencil to make their eyes darker and Grandad's quiff stand out a bit more. They both look happy. He turns away from the photo. That's when he sees what he has come for—the cardboard box for Uncle Freddie, resting on Nan's bed. He picks it up carefully and creeps downstairs.

With his hand resting on the door handle, he listens to them talking in the living room. There's still no laughter and it sounds a bit serious, but at least Nan isn't shouting. He pushes the door open and they all stop talking, mid-conversation. He can't tell if they're annoyed that he's there or if they're feeling sorry for him until, finally, Auntie Sandra says, 'Alright, our Jamie,' and he starts to feel okay again.

There is a soft *Ooooooooh* from everyone, except Grandad. Jamie puts the box down in the middle of the floor and lifts it out—his creation—a Boy George hairpiece of braided wool stitched into a black bowler hat. Each braid has been carefully woven with red, blue, and yellow ribbons, just like the one George had worn in the pop-video.

Auntie Sandra sits forward on her knees and touches

the hat, fingering the braids. 'Oh look, Freddie. Ain't he made a nice job of it? You're gonna look the biz. Look at all them ribbons. Must have taken him hours.' She looks at Jamie. 'Did you plait each one yourself?'

'Nan helped me get a few of them going. But mainly I did it myself.'

Nan is wiping away inky tears and smudges of green eye shadow. She sighs, 'I ain't been able to go for a piddle all afternoon.' She points at the living room door where Jamie had been working. 'He's had them plaits tied around the door handle and I daren't disturb the artist at work.'

Uncle Freddie smiles. 'I knew he'd make a good job of it. He's got the right sort of hands.' He carefully lifts up the hairpiece and tries it on. Everyone laughs. Jamie thinks it's a bit of an insult. He doesn't look a bit like Boy George. Not with that big, dark moustache. More like Freddie Mercury in a wig.

'Watch him, our Sandra! He might be on the turn.' Nan roars with laughter.

'What's *the turn?*' Jamie asks, and they all laugh again.

Then Uncle Freddie makes his voice feminine and high-pitched and says, 'I'd prefer a nice cup of tea.'

Auntie Sandra joins Nan in laughter—shrieking, in fact, but it sounds a bit forced, perhaps to make Uncle Freddie feel better about a joke that clearly no-one understands.

'He's a clever lad, our Jamie,' Auntie Sandra says, hugging him tightly.

Then there's another thump of a knuckle at the window and they all turn to look, even Grandad this time. 'That'll be y'mother,' Nan says. 'Jamie. Get y'coat.' She goes into the passageway to open the front door. 'Alright Gloria? Oh my God, you're wringin'.' She comes back into the room with Gloria behind her.

'Alright everyone?' Gloria says, standing in the doorway, in a two-tone blue batwing jumper. She always makes a dramatic entrance. 'It's coming down in sheets out there. I'm not stopping. Just come to pick the bab up.'

'Alright Glo?' they chorus.

She takes one look at Uncle Freddie and says, 'What in the world have you got on your head? Y'silly bugger.' She squeezes in and steps over Uncle Freddie's legs. 'Alright bab? You had a nice day?'

Jamie flings his arms around her. They hug. Then she pulls her nose up and glares at Nan. 'Mother! You been giving him whiskey again?'

Nan shrugs. 'Only a dribble. Help him sleep better.'

'Mother!' Gloria snaps again. Jamie has his head pressed into her neck but he knows she's making mean faces at Nan.

'Don't make a fuss, Glo,' Nan says, settling herself into her seat, plumping the cushions behind her.

Gloria lets go of him and ruffles his hair. The room is so small she's standing in between Uncle Freddie's outstretched legs to check herself in the wall mirror. 'My

hair's gonna go all frizzy now. I've only just had this perm.'
She teases wet curls with the tips of her fingers. 'Come on
Jamie. Get your stuff together. I've got to get back to get
y'dads tea on. Give everyone a kiss.'

Jamie already has his coat on and is moving to begin
kissing everyone goodbye. 'Love you, Nan.'

Nan leans forward and raises a cheek. 'See you soon,
cock,' she says. 'And don't take any notice of him.' She
points at Freddie. 'He's nothing but a bloody varmint. I'll
put one on him if he upsets you.' At the same time she
hands the afro-comb from the mantelpiece to Gloria.

'Bye Auntie Sandra,' Jamie says, leaning to kiss her.

'Mmmmmmwaa! See you soon, Bab.' Auntie Sandra
squeezes him firmly. She tickles his ribs. He struggles
to escape. 'You're hurting me!' He squeals. She lets go of
Jamie and he falls to the floor, squealing.

'I'll save you some more of them pictures,' Auntie
Sandra says.

'Bye Uncle Freddie.' Jamie moves to kiss his stubbly
cheek and Freddie squeezes him in his big muscly arms.
'See ya, Nancy Boy.'

The back of Gloria's hand comes down, crack! across
the back of Freddie's head, knocking the Boy George
headpiece to the floor.

Freddie's hand shoots to the back of his skull.

'I've told you not to call him that,' Gloria says.

'Christ Glo, you didn't have to hit me *that* hard.'

She flashes her teeth at him. 'You'll be speaking on the other side of your face if you say it again.'

'What's wrong with it? He's one of a kind, ain't he?'

Gloria fixes him with her eyes. 'Just carry on. I'm warning you.'

Jamie moves to Grandad. There's a cruel look in his eye. He raises the palm of his hand to Jamie. 'What is it with all this kissing?' he says.

Jamie is stunned. Grandad can barely look at him. Jamie doesn't know what to say. At the same time, he feels something tug on his leg. He turns and looks behind. The red wool from the knitting has snagged on his shoe and he's dragged lengths of it out of the bag and across the floor.

'Oh Dad, he always kisses you,' Gloria says. 'He's your *grandson*. Give him a kiss, for heaven's sake.'

Something has changed. He does always kiss Grandad when he's leaving. Jamie suddenly feels as if he's saying goodbye to them all for a very long time. It doesn't feel right. He's so very far away and so incredibly alone. Grandad should say something. He *is* his grandad after all. But he doesn't. His face turns to the wall. Deep lines curl away from his nostrils and his top lip disappears inside his bottom one. He seems to have lost interest in the Spitfire altogether and his sad, watery eyes are staring at the clock.

Jamie winds the wool back into the bag. 'Mum. What's wrong with—'

Gloria grabs him by the arm, as if there's something to be feared. 'Grandad's got a few things on his mind.' As she speaks, Jamie pulls out the partially knitted pencil case. 'Come on. I'm doing liver'n'onion tonight,' Gloria says.

He looks at the ruined work, red wool unravelling, stitches—loose from the needles. He can't for the life of him work out why Grandad has become so unfriendly, but he's sure it has something to do with the knitting.

# Yarn

Gloria's about to lock up for lunch. She places Mrs Hickingbottom's Sirdar order on the counter, ready for her to pick up, darts to the back of the shop to set the burglar alarm and then she's out the door, flipping the 'closed' sign as she goes. She peers through the glass, checking the shop she's managed part-time for years. She turns the key, locking inside happy memories. It was the first job she'd had since having little Jamie and sometimes, during holidays, he used to sit with her on the bottom of a stepladder—a knitting mascot for the old ladies. The lights are off. The soft, comforting balls of wool sit in rows of many colours inside wooden pigeonholes.

She makes a move into cheerful sunlight—across town, through the cemetery where they would all sit—Gloria, Jamie, Nan and Grandad—on the perimeter wall, eating potato fritters in batter, followed by a jam doughnut. She has to walk all the way home in these damned heels— bloody idiot, should have worn flats. There are the dogs to walk, the meat to take out of the freezer for Roy's tea and her lunch to eat. She's cutting it fine if she's to make it back early enough for the afternoon rush. It's always busy when the shelf-stackers from Kwik Save clock off after lunch and rush in to get their needles, patterns, yarn, or just stand gas-bagging. And today she's on her own. Margaret's under the doctor—peptic ulcer or some such trouble.

At home, she wolfs down her sandwich—cheese and

Branston—adds Jamie's school uniform to a pile of freshly ironed laundry and carries it up to his bedroom.

On the threshold she stands, scanning the room—bloody untidy bugger. 'Lord only knows what he gets up to in here,' she voices to the empty room. His desk is cluttered with paints and brushes. There's a wooden box with seashells glued to it and inside it's stuffed with letters and photographs. Next to the desk, an easel carries a piece of board he's painted a picture on—a spaceship flying across the cosmos. This is what he's into—science fiction and imagination. The walls are covered with pictures of now less-colourful pop stars—Boy George, washed-out, sadly lost in drugs, Holly Johnson lost behind the censors, and Freddie Mercury reportedly diagnosed with HIV, God love him. And there's Jamie's scrapbook—never grown out of it—big and red and bulging with cuttings.

She drops the basket of fresh washing on the floor, tidies the bed and arranges his teddy bears on the pillows. Then she hangs his clean laundry in the wardrobe, sniffing a school shirt—fragranced with fabric conditioner—and smiling inwardly. Fourteen and he's still her little boy.

The phone rings in the adjacent bedroom. 'Who's that now?' She dashes onto the landing, tripping over Roy's slippers, and into her own bedroom where she grabs the receiver. 'Hello?' From where she's standing, next to the window, she can see Mrs Tonks, waving up at her from the street, walking that daft miniature poodle—same route she does every day, wearing the same maroon cloche bucket hat.

'Oh, hello there. Is that Mrs Johnson?' comes a voice.

'Speaking.' If she's told Mrs Tonks once not to let that mutt urinate on the front lawn, she's told her umpteen times—piss burns ruin the grass.

'It's Annie—from the library.'

'Oh dear God,' Gloria says. 'Have we got overdue books? I thought I'd returned them?'

'No, no. It's nothing like that,' Annie says. 'It's about some books that Jamie's ordered through the inter-library loan service.'

'Go on.'

'Well, I've four books here. Art books. Paintings and such. They're ready for him to collect. Only I thought you'd better see them first.'

'Oh?' Gloria, turns away from the window now, one hand fiddling with her gold hooped earrings.

'Well, if it were my son, I wouldn't have a—I mean, it's not like he's—'

'Annie, what's our Jamie gone and done now?'

'I don't know how to put this. It's just that they're a bit, well, you know—*erotic*.'

Gloria pauses for a moment, absorbing what Annie's just said. 'Bloody Nora! You mean he's been ordering pornography?'

'It's nothing like that. I promise you.'

Gloria feels herself blushing. 'Dear God. What time are you open till?'

'Eight o'clock on a Thursday. It's my late night.'

'Right. I'll be in after work to vet them.'

'Alright Mrs Johnson.'

'Call me Gloria. Mrs Johnson makes me sound like an old woman.'

§

At the library Annie spreads the books out on the counter in front of Gloria. 'Do you see what I mean?'

Gloria flicks through the glossy pages of illustrations. Fantasy art they call it—Amazonian women wearing very little, voluptuous bodies, muscle-bound barbarians slaying dragons and sexy sorceresses riding winged beasts. She tries to keep her voice low. 'Some of this is quite tasteful, actually.'

Annie laughs. 'Mind you, you wouldn't want it on your bedroom wall, would you?'

'God no.' Gloria points at one female with an abundant cleavage. 'Enough to give you a complex.'

Both women titter, which draws a loud 'Shush', from behind one of the bookcases.

Gloria pulls a face and presses her lips together. 'I expect he's researching something. Our Jamie writes stories. Won a competition only last month. And he does a lot of drawing. Art's his favourite subject at school. Maybe he wants to copy some of these mythical creatures.' She exchanges a look with the librarian. There's an image of a muscular man seemingly being anally penetrated by a tree in the shape of a man, very artfully done, but —

Gloria bites her lip. She closes the book and looks at Annie. 'I'll make sure he doesn't take them to school.'

'I just wanted to be sure, Mrs... sorry... Gloria. Better safe than sorry,' Annie says. 'I'll just check these out to Jamie's account and you can take them with you, okay?'

§

In the dark, she's sitting on the edge of his bed, playing with his knitting bag, when he comes in from his after-school art class. She watches him through the bedroom door, coming up the stairs, alongside the slatted banisters, pulling off his school tie, and unbuttoning his shirt.

'Alright, Mum,' Jamie says, out of breath, as if he's been running. His voice is deep and slightly husky, in a way she'd never noticed before. When he reaches the top of the stairs he looks taller than she thought he was. Taller than his dad now. 'You checking my tension?' he says, leaning on the doorframe, the landing light behind him casting his face into silhouette, making him look a little gaunt.

'You still into this?' Gloria asks, thinking that she preferred it when he was.

'Not really. Grown out of it.' He gestures to his tube of paintbrushes. He walks in without switching on the light and places them on the desk.

She stands up. 'The librarian called today. I went to pick these books up for you.' She hands him a carrier bag with the books in. '*Art* they call it.'

'Oh, brilliant.' He reaches into the bag, excitedly. 'I've been waiting for ages for these.'

Gloria looks at her son—a furry shadow on his chin, Adam's apple, greasy hair, pimples—not so *little* anymore. Though he is thinner: she noticed when she was washing his clothes, he'd punched an extra hole into his belt. 'I know you only want to look at the tits!'

'Mum!'

'Your Dad says you'll go blind.'

'Mum!'

'I'm only saying.' She punches him on the shoulder and leaves him alone in the darkness of his room. 'If I catch you playing with yourself, I'll ban you from that library. Do you hear?'

# Mirror Ball

Ray's Volvo smells of warm plastic and lemon air freshener. It's all mock-luxury: leopard print seat covers and faux mahogany panelling. Jamie, his best mate—Paul, and Paul's sister—Debs are in the back. Angie, Paul's mum, is in the front passenger seat doing her hair. They're waiting for Ray, Paul's dad, to drive them all to the baths. They call it 'The Baths', but for as long as Jamie can remember the pool has been covered with a semi-permanent wooden dance floor. It's used for ballroom dancing now, and prom nights.

It's New Year's Eve and they're all going to party, just like they do every year. No school for another week. They're all dressed up. Paul and Jamie are in grey chinos, black slip-on shoes and cotton shirts. Jamie's is pink. Paul's is lemon. Debs is wearing a sequined dress with a lace over-skirt and mesh fingerless gloves.

As per usual, Ray is the last one to get ready. He sticks his head through the driver's side window. 'Angie, have you seen my gold bracelet? I can't find a stick of jewellery anywhere.'

'It's on the dressing table next to your cufflinks. And hurry up—we're gonna be late.'

He disappears again. Angie carefully divides her hair into sections with a comb and applies portable curling tongs that she's connected to the cigarette lighter. She looks over her shoulder. 'Looking forward to it, kids?'

'Highlight of my year, Mum.' Paul laughs and elbows

Jamie playfully.

Finally, Ray gets in, suitably bejewelled, patting his hair, quiff at the front, duck's arse at the back. His shirt is open to the fourth button down, revealing the flash of a gold chain and a mat of chest hair. He reeks of eau de toilette, but Jamie knows he must have rushed in the shower because there's still the undercurrent of armpit odour beneath cheap deodorant.

He throws his leather jacket at Jamie and says, "'Ere Cock, put that on the back shelf, will ya?' He pulls the plug of the heated tongs out, chucks it into Angie's lap, pushes the cigarette lighter back in and says, 'Have you got the tickets?'

'Ray! I was using that.'

'You look fine. Don't make a fuss,' he says, picking a cassette off the dashboard and inserting it into the player. He turns the rear-view mirror to face himself, licks a finger and smoothes down his eyebrows. Then, he adjusts his seat and belts up like a fighter pilot in an F-14 Tomcat.

As he turns the ignition, Angie says, 'Did you lock the back door?' and the car lurches forward to the sound of *Take My Breath Away*, nearly causing her to doodle lipstick over her cheek. She punches him hard on the shoulder. 'You left it wide open when you went out last Wednesday. That's why the place stinks of cat's piss. I come home to a kitchen full of stray moggies.'

Jamie's still trying to find room for Ray's jacket behind

him. The whole back seat shelf is cluttered with Debs' dancing trophies.

Angie hands two ten-pound notes over her shoulder. 'That's for your drinks, lads. Don't spend it all at once.' She didn't do that last year.

'Where's mine?' Debs says.

'Your Dad'll buy *your* drinks. You're not old enough.'

'Neither are these two. They're only sixteen.'

The lighter pops out again and Ray says, 'Angie, light me one of them cigars, will you luv.'

'You're a girl,' she says, ignoring Ray. 'I don't want you going near that bar. Understand?'

'It's not fair. You never let me do anything because I'm a girl.'

Jamie takes the tenner and puts it in his pocket. 'Thanks Angie.'

Angie turns around in her seat and looks directly at him. 'Jamie sweetheart, keep your eye on her, will you?'

'Alright Ange,' Jamie says. When Angie sits back, he nudges Debs. She looks at him and he puts a finger to his lips, tapping his trouser pocket at the same time. She smiles and touches her top lip with her tongue. Unbeknownst to Angie, Jamie and Paul have been doing extra paper rounds for beer money.

Angie turns round in her seat again. 'Here, Jamie, it might be your lucky night,' she says, perhaps a little too enthusiastically.

'How do you mean?' Jamie asks, feeling himself blush.

'You might meet your future wife,' she says.

Paul rolls his eyes and inspects his biceps.

Debs shakes her head. 'Are you kidding? At the *baths*?'

'It's where me and y'dad met,' Angie says.

'A marriage made in heaven,' Paul says.

'Pure Barbara Cartland,' Debs says, and looks out of the window.

At the baths, they pull onto the muddy car park where Alan, Janice and Darren are waiting at the bottom of the steps. They all get out of the Volvo—Debs runs to Darren and snogs him. Ray walks over to Alan, his drinking partner—they shake hands and slap each other on the shoulder.

'All right, mate?' Ray says and then turns to Paul and throws his car keys at him. 'Park it round the back, Son. And don't scratch it.'

Paul's eyes widen. 'Thanks Dad,' he says, watching them all walk up the steps to the dancehall. Angie and Jamie struggle behind with plastic bags of picnic food, soft drinks and undelivered Christmas presents. Her shoes are sinking into puddles.

Angie shouts to Ray, 'Do you really think you should be letting him park that car?'

'Why?' Ray asks.

'I only washed it yesterday. He's gonna drive it through all that mud.'

'Oh, stop going on, woman!'

From one of her carrier bags, Angie pulls a fire extinguisher sized canister of hairspray and mists her head as they go through the double doors. She passes it forward to Janice who does the same, walking down the corridor.

'Fuck's sake Janice!' Alan says. 'I can fucking taste the stuff. Leave it out.'

§

It's ten o'clock. The bar at the side of the dance floor is packed. Jamie's drinking cider, because it's all he can stomach. He hasn't yet acquired a taste for ale, like the other men. He's been buying double shots of Vodka in pint glasses of lemonade for Debs, so her Mum won't find out. Even Darren doesn't know. He's like the fucking thought-police, eager to score brownie points with Angie.

Paul's off sharking. Darren is talking to some older boys from school and Jamie is giving them all a wide berth, soaking up the smoky atmosphere. It's the kind of place that time left behind: beer-stained carpets and toilets that stink of sick.

The mirror ball sends a dotted trail of light along the wall. Jamie follows its path around the room until it crosses the faces of Ray and Angie, finishing their first dance of the evening. They're perfectly matched, height-wise. Short. Ray's in Cuban heels and Angie is wearing very gold, very high heels, and *now*, very shiny, since she's wiped off the mud with a tissue. They go well with the gold sequined frock she's wearing and her golden, shimmering, not-quite-finished hair-do.

The track comes to an end. 'Shit,' Debs says, getting all jittery. 'Mum's coming over.'

'It's alright. Remember, it's only *lemonade*.'

'Alright, me luvs,' Angie says, smoothing down her lamé skirt.

'Yeah,' Jamie says. 'Did you enjoy your dance?'

'Probably the last one I'll get. He's gone off to talk to Alan now, about a motor. You know what they're like. Ain't you found a nice girl yet?'

Angie is showing a lot of cleavage. She's wearing a pendant on a long gold chain, directing the eye deep into the folds of her sparkly dress.

'No,' Jamie says, lazily, and looks at Debs, who is rolling her eyes.

'Y'mum and dad didn't want to come, Jamie?' Angie asks.

He can just imagine his mother's face at the thought of it. When he left the house she was wearing a black and cream peplum jacket over a pencil skirt and pair of two-tone patent leather court shoes. And that's just what she throws on to run the vacuum cleaner round or walk the Alsatians.

'They're at home watching television. Dad's been working long hours lately.'

'They don't know what they're missing,' she says. 'Is he still roofing?'

He nods. 'I think he's doing all right. Can I buy you a drink, Angie?'

'You save your money, luv.' She lowers her voice and nods over to our table in the corner. 'Me and Janice have got a bottle of Vodka stashed.' Then she slaps Jamie on the shoulder and points a sharpened fingernail at him. 'You looking after *her*?' she asks, nodding at Debs, leaning sheepishly, behind him.

'Yeah, course.'

'More than I can say for that boyfriend of hers.' Angie folds her arms and looks around the room. 'Where is he?'

'He's talking to some of his mates,' Jamie says.

She looks at Debs. 'I thought I told you not to come near this bar?'

Debs pinches her face into a fake smile and holds up her glass. 'Lemonade,' she says.

'Even so. Why don't you go and have a dance with Jamie? You'd like that, wouldn't you, Jamie?'

Before he can decline, Debs says, 'Why don't you worry about Paul as much as you worry about me?' Jamie leans back against the bar, out of the firing line.

'Your brother can look after himself.'

'Really?' Debs says.

Angie turns again and looks over her shoulder. 'Where is he anyway?'

'Probably in the toilet selling something.'

§

Paul is unzipping his fly next to Jamie. Jamie looks at him out of the corner of his eye, as Paul liberates his undercarriage in strong, muscular hands. He lets out a loud groan of relief as a steaming flow of liquid hits porcelain. Paul rocks his head back, relishing this moment. Then he says, 'Alright, cock?' It's what he'd said to Jamie the first time they ever met. Jamie had been racing his radio control model car in a spot of wasteland called 'The Burn', a quarry, half-filled with rainwater, a short distance from where he lived.

A group of older boys from another school ambushed him and tried to steal the car. One boy, the tallest, had a mean look in his eye and blonde highlighted spikes in his hair. He'd started mouthing off at Jamie. 'That's ours now. Hand it over.'

The boy wrenched the car from Jamie's hands, pushed him to the floor and kicked him hard in the ribs. The boy was just about to make off with it when Paul appeared brandishing the butt of the snooker cue he always carried around. 'Go and play in the traffic,' he said. He put the control to his own car on the floor. The gang laughed at Paul, but when he went for them, showing no fear, swinging the cue hard enough to fracture a skull, they scarpered—the boy with Jamie's car letting it fall to the ground. Paul laughed and turned toward Jamie. Jamie had seen him at The Burn before, with his model car. They went to the same school but this was the first time he'd spoken to Jamie. Paul picked up Jamie's car, inspected it for damage. 'All in one piece,' he nodded to himself, holding out his other hand to help Jamie up off the ground. Jamie had felt tears stinging in his eyes. 'Don't let them get to you. Fucking low-life. We're in the same year, aren't we? I'm Paul.'

Jamie is staring down into the toilet trough now. He can't piss. Nothing. He bears down on his bladder harder, squeezing his abdomen. He closes his eyes in embarrassment.

'False alarm?' Paul asks.

'Something like that,' Jamie says, and feels his cheeks burning red.

'It's no wonder,' he says. 'Have you seen the birds in here? That one behind the bar—Linda Lusardi look-a-like—she's had me like a compass near north all night. I thought I was gonna have to piss standing on my hands.' Then he whistles. 'Fantastic tits,' he says. He exaggerates the consonants in 'tits', as if he really enjoys the sound of the word in his mouth. Jamie hears the guy on the other side of him grunt in agreement.

A stream of piss from between Paul's legs hoses down the porcelain. He moves away from the trough. Jamie hears the tap go on behind him and the sound of running water in the sink—suddenly he can go. He lets his eyes roll back in his head for a moment as the pressure of liquid, seemingly backed up somewhere inside his ribcage, releases like a lukewarm hot-water bottle being emptied down a drain.

Paul's hand is on his back. Jamie senses him playfully sniffing his neck. 'Mmm. Nice aftershave. Who are you trying to impress?'

Jamie laughs. 'Wouldn't you like to know?'

'Lock up your daughters,' Paul calls out to the toilet and giggles. 'Do you want another pint?' he asks, stepping away. Jamie glances over his shoulder at him, preening his curly dark brown hair in the mirror, muscles in his forearm flexing as he runs his fingers through his hair. Jamie hasn't heard him mention his radio-controlled car for a long time. Jamie nods acceptance of a fresh cider and then Paul leaves the toilet.

The guy next to Jamie at the toilet trough is pissing some kind of radioactive yellow fluid that makes Jamie think he might need a new set of kidneys. It trickles along the trough and merges with Jamie's relatively clear urine and collects in the drain cover, inches away from his toes, foaming up like Coca-Cola. Jamie turns his head for a second and snatches a look at him: old fella with a stoop, red face, broken veins on a purple nose.

Jamie shakes, zips himself up and takes a deep breath. The air is noxious. His head swims. He leans, almost touches the wall, but notices the decaying water pipe—

sweating rust and pushing through caked gloss paint. The look of it makes him shudder. Jamie steps backwards from the trough and moves to wash his hands in a grimy ceramic basin. He stares at himself in the mirror, ruffles his hair, loosens his tie and undoes a button. His skin is smooth, uniform in colour. He has a few spots, but nothing to worry about. He frowns at the soft down around his chin. He's not yet developed stubble, like Paul, but he is changing. He's slimmer, faster—like a whippet. Paul can beat him in an arm wrestle, but he doesn't read books. He's not interested in the world, or at least not Jamie's world. Jamie's eyes are brighter, more vital.

In the mirror he sees guys walking in and out of the toilet. Their eyes are different, dull beads of glass, set deep in their skulls, like something has been stolen from them. Jamie is determined not to become like them.

He walks out of the toilet and onto the dance floor. He sways to the music on his own. An old lady gives him a dance lesson. It's Ada, one of Ray's mum's friends. She teaches him the quick step, and he picks it up pretty quickly. Then he hears Ray's voice behind him. 'Who's he think he is? Lionel Blair?' It smarts a bit, because Jamie can't tell if he means it as a joke or not.

§

It's now eleven o'clock and Debs is on the stage doing a solo number. It's like this every year. She's won so many of those dance competitions for the district, she always gets asked to perform, just before they do the raffle—some modern dance routine to Whitney Houston: *I want one moment in time… When I'm more than I thought I could be… When all of my dreams are a heartbeat away…*

*The irony*, Jamie thinks. He's still here where time has stood still, where the highlight of the week is Sharon Moody's mid-week power-ballad night at The Winking Frog and if he's lucky, a joyride around the estate in the back of one of his older friends' cars. Same as last year and the year before.

He watches Ray making a fuss over Debs, telling everyone around him that it's his daughter on stage. It's laughable really, because Ray thinks she's made it. But Jamie knows better. She's just cutting her teeth. If Ray has his way, he'll have her in the back of a van, driving her around the country, singing and dancing in working men's clubs. That's not what she wants. She's a brilliant dancer, but it's history she's always liked at school.

From across the room, Jamie can see Angie and Janice standing together, arms folded, dots of reflected light from the mirror ball gliding across their faces. Janice is top to toe in silver. Together they look like a couple of second-rate game show hostesses. Angie is looking over at Ray, shaking her head. He looks annoyed. He beckons her to go nearer the stage, next to him, but she sticks out her tongue at him.

The room is hushed and all eyes are on Debs while she's dancing and there are a variety of *ooooohs* and *aaaahs* from the audience as Whitney reaches the key change and Debs segues into her final sequence. Ray is jubilant. It's like Torvill and Dean's Bolero all over again. Old ladies dab tears away from their eyes as they watch Debs. She pirouettes, cartwheels and spins across the stage, all the while twizzling a bit of pink ribbon on the end of a stick. Suddenly, it gets caught on her foot and she trips. Jamie looks over at Ray who now looks crestfallen. Unbeknown to him, the vodka and lemonade are getting the better of his daughter and she nearly topples off stage. She makes a professional, tits-and-teeth recovery just in time for Whitney's money-note and a rapturous applause. 'Stunning!' says one of the old ladies, as if it were all part of the routine. 'Bloody breathtaking,' says another.

Next, a stocky woman in a grey trouser suit and a gent's haircut steps up to the tombola. With fingers like sausages strangulated inside gold sovereign rings, she pulls numbers from it and calls them out. Each time she does, the amp shrieks with feedback and she tuts with annoyance, her big moment being spoilt. Anyone would have thought it was the Oscars instead of a raffle. Still, the audience are very excited about the prizes. Jamie's already checked them out—nothing anyone would really want to win: a bottle of bubble bath, a magnum of sparkling Perry, edible knickers, cuddly toy and a compact disc of *Love Songs from the Movies on the Pan Pipes*. Compact discs are all the rage but he doesn't have a player yet. Shame. His dad is a big fan of the pan-pipes.

One of Jamie's numbers is called and he collects his prize. The butch woman with the mic, hands over a bottle of Opium by Yves Saint Laurent. Ray falls about pissing himself. 'Are you gonna give it y'mum or wear it yourself?' he says.

After the raffle, the DJ puts on some slower music, so Jamie dances with Debs. They're the same height. Tall. They rest their heads on each other's shoulders. Jamie nuzzles the gold curls of her hair with his nose. They smell of hairspray and perfume. Nice. They fall around in the music, bathing in it, as if it were tropical water. The floor is dappled with tiny shards of mirror-light. She leans back to look at Jamie. For a second, she's not a girl, but a woman.

'I'm fucking drunk,' she says and bites her lip.

'I know,' Jamie says and they giggle. 'I thought you were gonna come off that stage on a stretcher.'

She pulls him close again. Over her shoulder, Darren is frowning at them. For a moment Jamie thinks he's going to walk over and get in between them, but as Darren steps forward Angie grabs his arm. Jamie can lip-read her saying 'Oi, no y'don't!' and then 'dance with me, face-ache.' She's all flirty-mumsy. But as he tries to step away again, she points a finger and shakes her head. And then, miraculously, they're dancing. The top of Angie's head comes just to where Darren's nipples would be.

'Do you love him?' Jamie asks Debs.

'Who?'

'Darren.'

'Are you mad?' she asks.

'Why d'you go out with him then?' Jamie asks.

'Dunno. What else is there to do in this hole?'

He remembers the time they first listened to Whitney together. He'd gone round to call for Paul but it was Debs who answered the door. 'He's gone out with one of his girlfriends tonight,' she'd said. 'But you can come in and talk to me, if you like.' They ended up getting burnt on her portable sun-bed, singing *Didn't We Almost Have It All* at the tops of their voices. And that's when he told her. Well, maybe he didn't tell her *anything*. She just knew.

He feels Debs' hands moving, down his back, over his bum.

'You've got a nice arse,' she says. He feels her fingers gently squeeze flesh through the seat of his trousers and he wonders, for a second, if her brother might have a firmer grip.

'Thanks,' he says.

'My mother would say, 'It's a waste. Good looking guy like you.''

'I know,' he says and he feels her kiss his neck. Feelings of discomfort and affirmation wash over him simultaneously. Jamie pulls away and cranes his neck, looking for Darren.

Debs looks at him quizzically. 'Where's me Dad?' she asks.

'He's over there, dancing with the woman from Woolworth's again.'

'He's not?'

'He is.'

§

It's five to twelve. Angie and Jamie are sat at their big table eating crisps. The remnants of smuggled party food, cold fatty sausage rolls, pork pies and potato puffs, lie scattered on a beer-swilled tablecloth.

Paul comes up behind Jamie and puts his arms around him. 'It's nearly time mate.' He's drunk. 'How many girls have you snogged?'

'How many have *you* snogged?' Jamie says.

'Four,' he says.

'Five,' Jamie lies.

'Nah! You're a dark horse, ain'tcha. What you got, that I ain't got?'

'Must be my aftershave,' Jamie says.

Paul smells good. Manly. Jamie breathes him in deeply. Paul moves away. 'You coming then?'

'Where?' Jamie asks. He looks round. He's got his arm

around some bird now. *Christ, what toilet did you scrape her out of?* It's mean of him but all the same, Paul doesn't have great taste.

'For a dance,' he says, pulling the girl onto the dance floor.

'Oh, yeah,' Jamie says. 'In a minute.'

What's all the fuss about? It's just another fucking year. Nothing changes. The world will still be the same tomorrow morning. If he has to dance with Paul's mum another year, at twelve o'clock, he's going to kill himself. No, really, he will. He'll kill himself. He looks across the crowded dance floor at Ray. He's not going to leave that woman alone.

Angie gets up and heads over towards them. She stubs her toe on the empty Vodka bottle that she and Janice have discarded. 'Fuck!' She pushes her way through the crowd and nearly goes over on her heel. Jamie can see her talking to Ray. There are raised voices for a moment, and then she's walking back. 'Lousy bastard!' he hears her say. 'Looks like it's me and you again, Cock. Come on, get your dancing shoes on.'

The music, it's the Nolans. Why couldn't it have been *It's Raining Men*? He forces a smile. He swallows, heaves his unfortunate carcass off the seat and takes her hand. She lifts their hands up high and they cross the floor like *Come Dancing* partners in the Blackpool Tower ballroom.

The room seems like a drunken merry-go-round, Jamie

in the centre, barely moving, all the dots of mirror-light shooting around the perimeter. He lets his eyes follow one, a glass butterfly in a hurricane, hitting people in the face. Ray is drunk, slumped over the shoulder of the woman from Woolworth's. Alan and Janice are two-stepping together. Darren is dancing with Debs, if you can call it dancing—he's got two left feet. Her eyes are glazed over. She looks like she's thinking, *get me the fuck out of here*, which is not far from what Jamie's thinking. Angie puts her head on his chest and they go round to the music. He fakes a smile, closes his eyes and dreams he might find something new and unexpected in the darkness.

Then, he feels something touch his crotch—just a brush at first, and then something grabbing hold. His eyes snap open. Angie's hands are on his shoulders. He wonders if he could've imagined it, but there's a furtive look in her eyes and she lets out a wicked cackle, fluid rattling in her throat. Why do middle-aged women think they can do this? No luck with their husbands, so they turn to the boys.

Jamie's head is swimming. He's looking at Paul snogging the toilet bird, strong, well-developed forearms wrapped around her. His hand is on her tit. Jamie wishes his hand were—

And suddenly, everyone is counting down... ten, nine, eight... the music stops... everyone has let go of their partners... Angie is smiling... they're all smiling gleefully... three, two, one, zero... and there's a flash of light, a loud explosion and thousands of bits of glitter falling on them from above and... HAPPY NEW YEAR... and there's that expectation of resolution and turning over a new leaf and everyone kissing each other. Beery men hold each other in headlocks and the room spins and everyone is still smiling and then suddenly Toilet Bird is in front of him—her breath, a mixture of fags and Pernod.

'Happy New Year,' she says and her open mouth and tongue come straight at him. His hands come up in front of him and he goes rigid. She's shocked and bristles at the rejection. 'Bender!' she says and walks away. And then it's Auld Lang Syne and they're all standing in a circle. Except he's mouthing some shit because he doesn't know the fucking words... and then it's just the light that engages him... fractured light, shooting in every direction. For a moment, in his eyes, everything is frozen. Only the mirror ball turns, Seurat-speckling faces. Alan and Janice are arm in arm. Ray and Angie are snarling at each other. Paul, the reason for him being there, is absent. No surprises. Debs and Darren are in a static clinch. He's kissing her full on the mouth, tongue down her throat, big brutish hands inside her blouse, except her eyes are looking directly at Jamie. And he knows, in that one moment, they're both thinking the same thing.

The room starts turning again. This time, something has changed. It's not the same this year. Next year he won't be here.

# Mandarins in Jelly

'Secrets,' Billy says.

Jamie has been listening to him prattling while he thumbs through an interiors magazine.

'One day, you'll know all mine, Soft Lad.'

Raising his head to face their reflection, Jamie reconnects with Billy, shirtless and tanned, smiling—both of them enclosed inside the full-length mirror. Billy covers the shoulders of Jamie's 1950s cream polka-dot shirt with tea towels. Jamie muses upon Billy's rats' tails and his own low sideburns: Jamie favours Britpop, while Billy is still holding on to grunge.

Billy takes a brush from Jamie's free hand and butters magenta dye into his bleached blonde side parting and deep fringe. 'This stuff stinks,' he says, and moves to open the window.

'There's only one person who knows everything about me,' Jamie says. 'Paul Fullbrook.' The magazine drops to the floor as Billy dispenses a bowl of pink gunk into one of Jamie's hands and a comb into the other. The two of them work in sync.

'Your mate who went to America?'

Unable to move or do anything else, Jamie let's his eyes move around Billy's childhood bedroom. It's covered with images of black and white movie stars: Gloria Swanson, Bette Davis, Greta Garbo.

'Keep still,' Billy says and taps him with the dye brush. 'What does he know that I don't?'

Jamie hesitates. 'It's possible he's so disgusted by what I wrote to him that he's decided never to speak to me again.'

Jamie feels Billy staring at him from the mirror, head tilted a little, as if he were soothing a troubled boy. 'Christ! We're not that different,' Billy says. 'We'll be just like your parents when we're older. We can get a mortgage and a couple of puppies—semi-detached in Leamington Spa and an obsession with interior design.'

'I don't think Paul would be offended by a bit of interior design. It's the other stuff I wrote.'

'Oh, I see. The *other* stuff,' Billy says, smearing more pink paint onto Jamie's head. 'It's not only gay men who like a bit of anal, you know.' Billy wipes pink dye from Jamie's forehead with a pad of cotton wool. 'I'd put money on it—your mother's had it up the arse more times than I've had hot dinners...'

Jamie glances at the open door, through to the landing at the top of Billy's mum's stairs. 'Keep it down a bit, will you.'

'Stop being such an apologist. This *is* nineteen ninety-five not nineteen forty-five,' Billy laughs. 'They can't lock us away anymore. I'd be more worried about what Gloria's going to say about your hair. You're going to look like a giant fuchsia.'

'My mother loves fuchsias. Patio's covered.'

Billy scoops up Jamie's fringe and combs it back. 'If she didn't know you were gay before, she certainly will now.'

'Careful,' Jamie lifts a hand to his eyebrow. 'You're going to get it in my eyes.'

'There,' Billy says. 'We have to wait for twenty minutes.'

Billy clears away his hairdressing tools and wipes down the little table cluttered with brushes, foils and bottles of peroxide and ammonia. 'So anyway, what did you write in this letter that was so scandalous?'

'Everything.'

'Everything?'

'Everything!'

Billy rolls his eyes. 'What possessed you?'

'I was lonely. I kept a lot in,' Jamie says. 'Things got better when I met you in London.' He looks at Billy's reflection—his head is angled to one side again. 'But when I started writing, well—'

'It just poured out.'

'I expect Paul's told everyone by now.'

Jamie hears the sound of the living room door opening downstairs. He flinches.

'It's only Mum,' Billy says, as her footsteps mount the stairs.

'You can stop your funny business.' Val appears at the bedroom door, holding two mugs of tea. She sets them down on top of the bookcase. Everything about her is relaxed from her functional boyish haircut and her sloppy grey sweater. She leans against the doorframe and looks at Jamie's hair. 'Jesus Christ! What fucking colour is that?

73

Anyone would think you two batted for the other side or something.' She grins.

'Or *something*,' Billy says, ushering her back out of the room.

'What's with the floorshow?' Val asks, indicating Billy's bare torso.

'Didn't want to get dye on my shirt.'

'But you didn't worry about my nice tea towels!' She flares her eyes at him.

'Get out.' He steers her out of the room. 'This is boy's business. Go on. Off with you.'

'Don't do anything I wouldn't do,' she calls back to Jamie.

'Leaves us plenty of scope,' Billy says and presses the door shut on her.

Jamie smiles, stands inelegantly, rearranges the tea towels on his shoulders and flicks on the radio in the middle of *Smells Like Teen Spirit* by Nirvana. 'Paul Fullbrook. Jesus! Paul loved this.' He sits again in the chair they'd borrowed from the kitchen. 'We watched films together. Nothing else to do in Welston, so we used to walk the best part of two miles to the cinema together and get drunk on White Lightning on the way home. When I started at St Martin's, I hadn't heard from Paul for ages. Then his letter landed on the doormat in my digs; it came out of the blue. Mum had forwarded it from home. I was really surprised when I heard he was in America. Always thought he'd join the family building firm. He was working in a summer camp for teenagers.'

'And?' Billy sighs impatiently.

'The letter: details of the many shags he'd had, list of clubs he knew, parties he'd been to, the substances he'd used... everything you're supposed to do on your first flight away from home. And questions... *Fallen off the face of the Earth, Jamie? Forgotten how to use a pen? I know there's something you're not telling me.*'

Jamie feels Billy's hand on his shoulder. 'So you took this as an invitation to spill the beans?

'That stuff had been fermenting for years.'

'Meaning?'

'I'm twenty and only now experiencing the kind of starry-eyed relationship that people like Paul Fullbrook formed in their early teens. He was a girl-magnet. Probably lost his virginity at twelve.' Jamie smiles into the mirror. 'Before I met you, it felt like part of me hadn't been born.'

There's a knock at the door. Jamie stiffens.

'I'm going to the fish'n'chip shop,' Billy's mum calls. 'I thought we'd have a treat before you go back to London. Do you two want your usual?'

'Yes please,' Billy says.

'Are you two coming out?' Billy's mum shouts. 'Or are you going to stay in there and play with each other all night?'

'Fuck off,' Billy shouts back.

'You don't fancy a battered sausage then?' Her footsteps can be heard on the stairs again.

Billy shakes his head and turns to Jamie. 'I suppose writing to your mate felt cathartic.'

Jamie nods. 'We'd been close at school, during sixth form. There was no one else to tell. And the States seemed so far away. At least I didn't have to look him in the eye and say it.'

'It.'

'Yes, *it*,' Jamie says.

'Are we really worth so little, it has to be whispered?'

Jamie laughs. 'I didn't whisper. I evacuated my bowels onto the page. Everything came out. I wrote about the tantalizing, twilight excursions I'd had to the parks and toilets and canals of London.' Jamie remembers every word vividly. *Imagine a derelict tram-shed littered with intravenous needles, crack pipes and foils, left by junkies, and bottles of amyl-nitrate discarded by seekers of furtive nocturnal pleasure. We had sex in the dark. The only sounds were our grunts and the skitter of broken glass beneath our feet. Hardly glamorous but it was exciting to do something that has a sense of the forbidden—outdoors, public, under the moonlight.* 'I wrote about the porn, the dates, the drugs, the many, many men… I wrote about you.'

'Jesus! You told him all that?' Billy turns to face him in the chair. 'Not as green as I thought you were.'

'I don't expect Paul had ever read anything like it.

I wrote about The Black Cap in Camden and the drag queen, Regina Fong.' *The last of the Romanoffs. A Russian princess who fled to Britain after the revolution. Some of the other students and I go every week to see her lip-synching to scenes from Coronation Street and Are You Being Served? She's wicked. One night I got right next to the stage, close enough to pull her skirt and get her attention. She said, 'You touch these silks again and I'll put my stiletto heel straight through your fucking skull.'*

Jamie fingers an itchy patch on his head where the dye has started to burn. 'I wrote about my initiation into a new world. It wasn't poetry. But my god it felt good to get it out. Chapter and verse splurged onto that thin blue airmail paper—I kept accidentally making holes in it with the nib of my pen. Ironic, isn't it—the burden of so many years carried by that frail, weightless paper.'

Billy pulls Jamie out of the chair. For a moment their faces are so close together, their lips almost touch. Jamie lifts a hand and it lands on Billy's dewy abdomen, the way it had when they first met. After just a year in London, during an excursion to a nightclub, he had discovered Billy, a lad who, studying one year behind him at St Martins, had shared one vital peculiarity; they both hailed from neighbouring nowhere towns in the Midlands.

Cliques of clones in leather S&M harnesses held G&Ts as if they were standing around at an afternoon barbecue. Dancing cadavers mingled with muscle men transformed by steroids: gym-fit, hairless and tanned had become the prevalent fashion, perhaps to disguise the disfiguring effects of AIDS and antiretroviral drugs.

Jamie was the only guy still wearing a shirt, rocking his head to the trance music he couldn't abide. He felt insignificant next to their swollen bodies, chests and arms pumped like inflatables, nipples like rivets. He wished he occupied more space in the universe. He couldn't wait to get out of there.

Through a mosaic of airbrushed centrefolds, a young man moved towards him. He was toned and striking but not plasticized like the others. It couldn't be, thought Jamie. His naked chest was partially scribbled with unfinished tattoo. Peeping from underneath a blue and white denim baseball cap, his dark brown hair was dappled with an unbecoming orange. But Jamie knew. It was *him*. The one. Why there? Why then, in that place? And why that *orange* hair?

Jamie bundled deliberately and drunkenly into his path.

'Watch it,' the man said, steadying Jamie with both hands, preventing him from tumbling.

'Sorry,' Jamie replied, straightening his back and lengthening his vowels. 'Dancing. I wasn't looking where I was going.' He looked into the man's sparkling eyes.

'Mind on other things?' the man said, releasing him from his grip.

'I was just leaving.' Jamie smiled, perhaps a little too

flirtatiously. 'Maybe you could help me. I... need to get my coat.'

'What do you want me to do about it?' the man said.

'This place is so big. Cloakroom. Do you know where it is?' Jamie asked.

'Over there.' The man pointed. 'Up the stairs. Next to the bar.'

Jamie was still gazing into his eyes. 'Over there. Up the stairs. Next to the bar.'

'Yeah.'

Jamie recognized those flattened vowels anywhere. 'You're from the West Midlands? I'm from Welston.'

The man winced. 'You noticed, even in this din.' He wasn't going to be drawn in. He arched his neck to see above the bobbing heads.

'I'm Jamie.' Jamie beamed and extended his hand, trying to make himself more noticeable.

'Billy,' the man said and they shook hands. He smiled and gently moved Jamie out of the way. For a moment their faces were so close together, their lips almost touched. Jamie lifted a hand and it landed on Billy's abdomen. Billy gave him a condescending smile, as if he were an adolescent trying to prove he fitted in.

'Wait!' Jamie said. 'When am I going to see you again?'

Now passing him and slipping back into the crowd, Billy looked over his shoulder. 'You're not.'

'Love the shirt,' Jamie called after him.

Billy looked down at his naked torso. 'Thanks.' He smiled and vanished.

It wasn't until almost a week later that they bumped into each other again whilst perusing the sex toys in the basement of *CloneZone*. That's when they exchanged phone numbers. Jamie had been in London longer but it was Billy who knew the city better. Right now, Jamie would still be tortured by eternal dissatisfaction if Billy hadn't eventually wrenched him into the sewery depths of Soho, where they found solace amongst vintage-clad sexy boys. Week after week, they danced dreamily to Placebo and Pulp and Morrissey and Blondie at *Poptarz*. They cruised, they hooked up, they found possibility on the dance floor, but it wasn't long at all before they found themselves falling in love with each other and Jamie had taken Billy back to his digs, where they made the beast with two backs, over and over.

Jamie stares into Billy's eyes. Billy wrinkles his nose. 'So, you sent it?' He kisses Jamie gently, careful not to touch the strands of dyed hair.

'You know what I'm like. I almost didn't. I stood at the post-box for ages before watching the little chevrons of the airmail envelope fall into its cavernous red belly.' He throws his eyes up and slides his palms together, as if brushing away cobwebs.

'He's not written back?'

Jamie shakes his head. 'And Mum hasn't mentioned any

mail for me.' He walks to the mirror.

'You have your mail sent back home?'

'Post at the YMCA is hardly reliable. In between terms, post often gets lost.' Jamie inspects his eyebrows, wondering if they should be pink too.

'You'll see your mum before we go back to London. You can ask her.'

'She'll be looking forward to seeing you again,' Jamie remarks.

'She adores me. Must we keep up this pretence of us being *best friends*? I'm so obviously not your best friend.'

Jamie lowers his head. 'That mate of yours, Les— does he still want to take us to that gay bar?' Jamie asks, deliberately changing the subject. 'I didn't know gay bars existed in Welston.'

Billy wiggles pink stained, latex covered fingers at Jamie. 'The provinces never cease to amaze me.'

'Remind me how you know Les?' Jamie asks.

'He managed a shop where I worked.'

Jamie inspects his eyebrows again. They *should* be pink. 'I expect he is living it up in some New York nightclub.'

'Who? Les?'

'No. Paul Fullbrook. Probably surrounded by girls. Fuck, he had bad taste—Pamela Anderson types with fake *everything*. What Paul thought of as *feminine*, I always thought of as drag.'

Jamie leans forward, peers at his reflection. 'I think this

has been on long enough now. Shall we go and wash it off?'

Billy picks up two bottles—one shampoo, the other conditioner. 'Yes. Come on, I want you to fuck me with pink hair.'

'Animal!'

§

Under luminous clouds passing in front of a halogen moon, men shuffle between ramshackle buildings of corrugated iron and zigzag-roofed factories. This is the canvas into which Jamie steps—a jigsaw area, missing segments, parts shattered by economic decline. Outside a blacked-out doorway, more men loiter, waiting to be allowed in.

Les and his boyfriend, Mark, are bickering over what colour floor tiles they should have in the new conservatory. Billy is taking photographs with a new camera. Jamie rolls his eyes at Les. 'I thought *you* were supposed to be introducing us to this den of iniquity.' Shaking his head, he reaches and presses a buzzer painted with gelatinous black gloss. A little hatch opens in the door. Jamie turns and throws a surprised look at Billy. The gay bars and clubs of London are not secret or underground. Their names are scribbled in shouty bold colours and bright neon— *Heaven, Freedom, Compton's*. Yet here they are, Jamie and Billy, displaced and dispossessed, at The Pink Flamingo, too fearful to kiss or hold hands, standing outside a bar with no windows, waiting for the voice of a bodiless mouth to invite them in.

'Been here before?' the voice asks, sharp and waspish. Jamie has not but gives an affirmative reply anyway. 'You know what kind of bar this is, yeah?' Again, he nods. And finally, 'This is a bar for gay people and their friends. Any trouble and you're out! Understand?' Jamie nods once more. The door swings open and they're in. A contrasting world of colour and exultant popular music is found inside. The figure behind the door is, to Jamie's surprise, revealed to be a boy he knew from school, who was also bullied and ostracized from the others. He says, 'Alright Bab,' and Jamie nods, wondering if the lad recognises him or not as he points to Billy's camera. 'No pictures.'

'Oh?' Billy says. 'We were only going to take pictures of us lot.'

'Sorry Bab, management policy. You'll have to leave it here and pick it up later.'

They pass on through the entrance hall into a room decorated in nicotine-stained flock wallpaper, a mock-Flemish chandelier and a standard lamp with a tasselled shade. There's a video jukebox belting out camp classics and Eurovision hits. The clientele, whom Jamie senses all know each other, snap their heads round to look in their direction. *Know each other?* They've probably all *fucked* each other. Not much on the menu and so, it seems, Jamie and Billy are the new dishes on offer.

'I'll get the drinks,' Billy says, walking away, leaving Jamie standing with Les and Mark. All around him, a surreal scene for this area of Welston: young lads sitting with each other, holding hands—some of them kissing, lesbians playing pool, a woman smoking a cigar, two muscly, tattooed guys leaning over a fruit machine. Jamie never expected to find *this* on the edge of the council estate, where he grew up.

'We've just bought a place together,' Les says, sliding alongside Jamie onto a banquet behind a small rectangular table. 'One of those new starter homes, up in Bushbury. We couldn't afford much until the divorce comes through...'

Mark, settling into a wooden Admiral chair, is nodding, urging Jamie to sanction this plan. 'Obviously, he's still paying maintenance for the kids. So the decorating has been put on hold for now.'

'Though, having said that,' Les adds, 'We've just booked a cruise. Mark's always wanted to go to the Seychelles. I said, babe, if you want to go. Let's go.'

Part of Jamie feels envious. To be like his mother and father, to fall in love and, when the relationship tires, to work at it—is that the right thing to do? Though he also knows one of the benefits of being of his disposition is that you don't have to choose that model. A lifestyle can be invented—one that doesn't involve children or the Monday to Friday grind.

Jamie looks at Mark. 'You do know, I think, in the Seychelles, you can go to prison for being gay.'

'Oh, it'll be fine,' Les says, slipping out of his glittery Buck Rogers jacket. 'We're very discreet.'

On the other side of the smoke-filled bar, Billy is pulling notes from his wallet and handing them to a bald, fat man whose fingers glint with gold sovereign rings—a man who Jamie instantly recognizes. It's the fella who lives in the council house next door to his grandmother. He'd lived all his life with his mother, now dying of lung cancer. Jamie remembers him in the back yard, seen across the picket fence, hanging out washing with wooden clothes pegs in his teeth. The phlegmy rasp of his decrepit mother would call, 'Fetch us a cabbage from the yard, our Brian,' and he would point his eyes skyward, pick up a trowel and retrieve the vegetable. Now, with those same fat bejewelled fingers, he hands Billy his change with the grace of a gull swooping from the sky to catch a fish. Brian's eyes follow Billy, carrying drinks back to the table, until he and Jamie lock eyes; Brian winks with warm-hearted recognition.

Les draws hard on his cigarette and stubs it out in an ashtray. 'I'm dying for a piss.' Les stands, moves around the back of Mark, letting his hands fall over his shoulders and chest.

'Alright. Les!' Mark says, swatting away his groping hands. 'Go to the toilet then.'

Les looks hurt as he heads to the gents'.

'Jesus Christ! He's suffocating me,' Mark says, as Billy falls into the seat next to Jamie. 'I can't fucking breathe.'

Billy lifts his beer and holds it up to Jamie. 'Come on, let's get pissed.'

'Cheers.' Jamie winks at Billy and they clink glasses.

A crowd of gay boys and lesbians are arriving, some from home, after hours of getting ready, some from the office, the factory, the hospital, still in their work clothes.

Jamie watches the meaty tattooed couple snogging against the fruit machine.

'Fucking hot,' Mark says, rubbing the fabric of his crotch where an erection stirs and looks at Billy. Billy punches Jamie, affectionately, on the shoulder. 'So, what have I missed?'

Jamie let's out a little chuckle of solidarity for Mark. 'Les was telling me how content he and Mark are together now that they have fully assimilated. Cruise holidays and all. Proper little marriage made in heaven.' Jamie kisses Billy on the cheek. 'That could be us, one day.'

Mark looks away. 'I don't know what the hell I've let myself in for.' He lifts his beer and slugs.

Billy smiles. 'You're not going to elope and adopt a couple of orphans?'

'Told him a thousand times. I want to do something with my life before I settle down. And anyway, he already has kids.'

Jamie frowns. 'Isn't it a bit late to be saying that?'

'Les bought the house, not me. He goes on and on until I find myself going along with him. I never wanted to move in. It was just meant to be a bit of fun.'

The room is filling up now and Brian, the barman, flounces across the floor and opens up the second room, from which spills an effluence of pop music and dry ice. The crowd begins to peel off through the doorway towards the shimmering mirror-ball light.

'Have you thought of leaving him?' Billy says, warily. Jamie jabs him hard in the ribs.

'You like it here?' Mark asks, abruptly as Les exits the toilet.

Jamie nods. 'I never imagined this could be right on Mum's doorstep. Even if I'd known about it when I was growing up, I'd have been too young to explore it.'

Les is back at the table. 'Not bad eh, Jamie? I don't suppose it rivals your fancy London clubs.'

'It's this or the Bricklayer's Arms,' Mark says.

'Oh, the *Layers*,' Jamie says. He remembers being dragged there with Paul Fullerton and glimpsing the married men taking advantage of a dimly lit car park, skirts hitched up around their mistress' waists, knickers around their ankles. 'Isn't the Glasshouse Sauna more your thing?'

'The *Gentlemen's Health Spa*? Prowling around in nothing but a towel?' Les looks at Mark. 'No. We're strictly monogamous. Aren't we, Mark?'

Jamie looks at Billy and catches him rolling his eyes.

Jamie knows the sauna from an advert he'd seen in a magazine. He's never bucked up the courage to try but now he's with Billy—who knows?

Over Les' shoulders, the tattooed boys are still snogging. What might they do for a living? This is not Soho. This is not The Black Cap in Camden. Typical occupations taken up by gayers—make-up artists, magazine editors, art directors—are few and far between here in the Midlands. These men are more likely to be shift workers at a local factory. Jamie fetishizes the idea in his head—the smell of engine oil, the dirt and the grease that his father used to scrub down with astringent Swarfega.

Jamie exchanges a look with Billy, then glances at Mark and realizes they are all captivated by the same image of constructed masculinity. Les jumps out of his seat, postures—hands clasped behind his head, in an exaggerated pretend yawn—a display so distracting it draws them from the floorshow.

Mark throws his eyes up, knocks back his beer and stands up. 'Who's coming for a dance?' He looks at Billy.

Les sits again. 'My feet are killing me. We've been walking around IKEA all day.'

Mark snatches Les' silver Buck Rogers jacket and flings it at him. 'And who's fault is that?'

The dance floor, populated by a group of guys who look like they might go home to their wives at the end of the night, is a small square of dirty plastic releasing an acrid fragrance left over from a dirty mop. Jamie finds himself dancing next to Les, to some ridiculous genre of high-energy pop.

'So, you're up from London to see your folks?' Les shouts over the din.

Jamie nods. 'Couple of nights at Billy's mum's... then I'm having a night at my parents'—'

§

The following morning, Jamie steps into his mother's kitchen after a quick trip to see Phyllis. He pulls off his shoes and calls out, 'I'm home!'

On the kitchen work surface is a glass dessert bowl full of partially-set orange jelly with pieces of fruit floating in it, like suburbanites in suspended animation.

'I made your favourite pudding.' It sounds like an accusation.

'So I see.' He turns to see his mother in the living room, runs one hand through his newly-dyed hair and holds out a bouquet in the other. Gloria is staring at him as if she has just caught a stranger stealing money from underneath his grandmother's mattress. 'You and I need to talk,' she says coldly and heads upstairs.

'Alright, Son.' Roy, in his usual inert manner, dips the newspaper resting on his paunch and peers over the rims of his reading glasses. 'Nice hair.'

Jamie frowns. 'What's got into her?'

Roy shrugs and returns to his paper, as Jamie follows Gloria upstairs. They sit on the bed that used to be his. All his posters are gone. She changed the wallpaper after his first three months at university. Now, everything is pink and floral—matching his hair. Her hands smooth down the bedclothes.

From behind her, like a magician pulling a white rabbit from a hat, she produces a letter, pale blue in colour with holes in it made by the nib of a pen, held between trembling fingers. In her other hand—an envelope. Red and blue chevrons around the edge. Jamie's mind frantically retraces imaginary steps across the Atlantic. Jamie's letter to Paul sent months ago—opened by a complete stranger, noted *not for me* by the recipient and readdressed to the address at the top of the page. She begins to read, '*It was the danger of it that was most thrilling. I could smell what he wanted. We only stood at the urinals, staring at each other for a few moments, before he was leading me by the hand, into a toilet cubicle where we clumsily, eagerly wrenched belt buckles, tore at shirt buttons, unzipped flies to hold each other's—*'

'Stop!' Jamie cries. 'Stop!'

'Is it true?' she snaps, throwing the letter down onto the bed and staring now at his plumage of pink hair.

He doesn't need to answer. This isn't coming out. This is falling out. This is worse than being caught in a public toilet by a policeman.

No one ever wants their mother to read *this*—the forensic report of her son's other life, now drawn to a dramatic denouement. He can see it all on her face. The questions. The assumptions. *Are you being safe? Are you going to die of AIDS? I'll never have grandchildren.* What she says is: 'Don't tell your Dad.'

'Why?' Jamie asks, bluntly.

Silent for a moment, she jerks her chin back into her neck, as if the question is a confrontation he ought not to be making. Regardless, he holds his gaze. 'Well,' she says, 'We don't know how he'll react, do we?'

Now the secret is out, Jamie doesn't see any point in keeping it from others. 'What do you think he'll do?'

'I don't think he'll break open the champagne, if that's what you're thinking.'

§

From Billy's clapped-out Vauxhall Nova, Jamie looks back at the house where he's spent the night—a modest suburban semi with its square front lawn, its conifers and rosebushes all neat and tidy, just like his parents. The silence of the neighbourhood is deafening—no dogs barking, no police sirens, no noisy public transport.

Billy laughs. 'Don't tell me. She's gone off fuchsia?'

On the verge of tears, Jamie stares into the mirror mounted inside the passenger side sunshield—eyes as pink as his hair.

'Come on, let's get out of here,' he says, and suddenly sobs into his hands.

'Hey, what's wrong? What's happened?'

'I can't tell you here,' Jamie cries. 'I just want us to get away.'

Billy drives, passing rows and rows of houses, neatly delineated by regimented flowerbeds and neatly mown lawns—each of the houses an imitation of the others with their tidy TV aerials, their garage doors, and their floral displays in a bay window. After half a mile, Billy parks up on the side of the road. 'We can't drive all the way back to London like this. You have to tell me what's happened?'

Jamie takes a deep breath. Billy undoes his seatbelt, turns and touches Jamie on the cheek. 'It's all right, Soft Lad. This is *me*. Just tell me.'

He covers his eyes with a hand. 'I *knew* there was something wrong.'

'Oh god!' Billy says. 'She's not ill, is she?'

Jamie thrusts the letter into Billy's hands—pale blue in colour with holes made in it made by the nib of a pen.

'Jesus! This is—'

'Yes.' Jamie hangs his head.

'Bugger me!'

Jamie sobs. 'I think it's buggering that's got me into all this trouble.'

Billy laughs. 'So you've come out?'

'Not entirely.'

'What do you mean?'

'She said, 'Don't tell your Dad.''

'But you *did* tell him?'

'No.'

'Why not?'

'She said, 'If you tell your father, he'll throw a fit. You know what he's like. I'll end up coming down on your side and then we'll have to get a divorce.''

Billy lets out an angry gasp. He slams his hands on the steering wheel.

'She said she'd made my favourite pudding. As if that would make it all better. Can you imagine? I haven't wanted mandarins in jelly since I was ten.'

'Fuckers!' Billy is suddenly red in the face. 'Fuck them! This kind of thing makes my blood boil. You go through school being beaten black and blue, picked on, called names, spat on. If you can get through that you've done well. But then you finally build the courage to tell your folks—the people who are supposed to love you, protect you, nurture you—about this essential part of yourself, that is by now malformed and unnourished, only to find it's a truth so unpalatable to them, so beyond their comprehension that they ask you to keep it a secret to save their sham of a marriage.'

'Billy, calm down. This isn't helping.'

'I'm sorry. This has hit a nerve. You're basically told

repeatedly that you're a reject, that it's something that must be whispered in corners. It's no surprise guys think so little of themselves that they throw themselves into alcohol, drugs, meaningless and dangerous sex. Ha! And they wonder why there's a fucking AIDS epidemic. Well fuck them!' Billy belts up and slams the car into reverse.

§

'I'm sorry boys, we don't really have time for this. We're off to the *Scan'n'Pack*.' Gloria's heavily plucked brows arch so high that her usual startled appearance is almost a touch *Divine*.

'Go on then,' Billy says. 'Tell him!'

Jamie stands at the edge of the room shifting his weight from one leg to the other on Gloria's burgundy Axminster.

'Tell him what?' Gloria asks, the tips of her curls twitching maniacally.

'Gloria?' Roy appeals, shaking his car keys—the soft wrinkles below his grey, receding hairline pleading with her. Jamie wonders if his own hair will one day thin and ebb away.

'I won't be forced into this,' she says. 'You can't just come in here shouting the odds.'

Jamie clutches Billy's elbow. Roy has noticed this action and peers at his son, tilting his head a little.

Jamie looks at Billy's hard face staring at Gloria. 'This

is not your story, Mrs Johnson.' Her eyes are wet now and she's trembling.

Jamie breathes deeply, an electric chill running down his neck, hair follicles all over his body standing on end.

'Roy—Jamie wanted to tell you something. Something honest and truthful and good. And *she* wants him to keep it a secret from you.'

'Jamie?' Roy says.

'Dad,' Jamie says. Jamie's hand tightens on Billy's elbow. Billy's face softens. 'It'll be alright.'

Finally, she breaks. 'You'd better sit down, Roy.'

Roy flops onto the leather sofa. 'I hope this isn't going to take long. She's given me a list of jobs to get through.'

Gloria sits next to him, resting her hand on his knee. 'Now Love, this might come as a bit of a shock to you. I don't want you getting upset.'

Roy folds his arms defensively over a slight paunch stretching the bottom of his baby blue polo shirt. 'Whatever it is, I'm ready.'

'It's just that, well... you know... Billy and Jamie... you know how you thought they were best friends... Well—'

'We're not best friends, Dad,' Jamie says. His fingers curl around Billy's hand. Billy squeezes them tightly. 'We're—'

'Is that it?' Roy looks at them all, as if they've all gone completely mad. 'God I thought someone had died.' Roy gets up walks into the kitchen. Jamie can't look at the other two. He finds himself staring at Gloria's faux

Grecian plaster fireplace. There's the sound of the fridge door opening and closing and he comes back with a pack of four beers. He hands one each to Jamie and Billy, snaps off the ring-pull on his own and raises the can up. They, all three, touch beers together, making a dull springy noise. He shakes his head at Gloria and chucks the last beer into her lap. 'So do you still want to go shopping then?'

§

'It's over.' Billy's hand falls onto Jamie's leg as he changes into fourth gear.

'I felt invisible,' Jamie says. 'How can something that's about me, suddenly become *her* drama?'

'It's done now.' Billy accelerates towards the brow of the hill on the outskirts of Welston.

Jamie lays a hand over the top of Billy's fingers. 'I love you.'

The sky above the trees and houses is layered with globular masses of clouds suspended in sunset, under which Jamie and Billy turn towards the motorway slip-road, London bound.

# Trifle

Phyllis works a good look: a whale-blubber slick of pearlescent pink bleeding into wrinkles, antique brooch with headscarf, emerald green eye shadow. She scrubs up well, especially at Christmas. Today, the pearls and clip-on earrings have come out. Everyone thinks she's frail, with her angina and her watery eyes, but she's got anti-corrosive in her blood and radiator sealant in her bladder—nothing wrong with *her* waterworks. Gloria always says, *She'll outlive us all.*

'Merry Christmas, Nan,' Jamie says.

'Give us a cuddle.' She walks in, arms wide, like a Mafioso boss, pulls him to her tightly and whacks him on the back as if winding a baby. 'Hardly get to see you these days. Bloody defector. Where's your mother?'

'She's doing the dinner,' Jamie says.

Phyllis lets go of him, smacking her lips together. 'Something smells nice.' Then she looks at the music-centre. Doris Day sings *White Christmas*. 'I love a bit of Doris Day at Christmas. It's traditional, ain't it.' Her eyes sparkle a little. Jamie joins in while she sings along. 'Her and Rock Hudson—they used to call 'em *Hollywood's Golden Couple*. A fairy tale made in heaven.' Jamie smiles. 'I used to do my hair like her, but it was always too dark.' Phyllis turns, sprightly, arms spread, ready again to guide and usher Alf to safety. 'I've brought the invalid with me. We've had back-to-back Max Bygraves all morning at our place. *You're a Pink Toothbrush, I'm a Blue Toothbrush*,' she says. 'Come on, get him in.' She points at Alf in the doorway where she's left him and then at the armchair, as if instructing removal men with a piece of furniture.

Alf shuffles in, leaning on his walking stick, struggling with two plastic carrier bags full of Christmas presents. 'Alright, Grandad,' Jamie says over Phyllis's shoulder. He moves around her to take Alf's arm and help him lower himself into the armchair by the window. He's more cheerful than usual. The walking stick and the bags of presents crash to the floor, like rubble from a crane grabber, as the bulk of him finally makes contact with the seat.

'Alright, our Jamie,' Alf says, squinting at Jamie through lenses the thickness of a glass ashtray. 'How're things down in the Big Smoke?'

'Oh, fine, y'know,' he nods, hoping for no further inquisition. They don't talk about what happens in *The Big Smoke*. In fact, Jamie and Alf haven't made proper conversation for years. Alf would usually be in one room with the men watching the football. Jamie would be in another with the women watching *Emmerdale Farm* on the portable.

'Making a go of it down London with that mate of yours. Ah, doin' well for himself, ain't he, Phyllis?' Alf says. Phyllis's attention is elsewhere.

'I'm coming to the end of my degree. I'll be looking for a job. So hopefully, we'll have enough money to get a flat,'

Jamie says, trying his best to sound as if 'best friends' set up house together all the time.

'How long are you here for?' Alf asks, rearranging himself in the armchair.

'I go back the day after boxing day,' Jamie says.

Roy comes in from the kitchen, pulling up the sleeves of his Aran—the one Gloria knitted for him. 'What can I get you two to drink?' he asks, despite the fact that they are both still in their coats. He goes to Alf and struggles to get him out of his sheepskin while he is still in the armchair. 'Lift up Alf, and I'll get it off you.'

Phyllis has been looking over Jamie's shoulder at the display of Christmas cards on the mantelpiece. Gloria's trying to transform this two-bed semi into a national treasure. She likes *traditional*—false oak beams and fake leaded windows. She likes white weddings and meat and two veg. She likes fish and chips on a Friday and wash-day is always Monday. She likes brown sugar in her coffee. She likes Catherine Cookson novels and floral curtains.

'*To a Special Couple?*' Phyllis remarks and makes a bee-line for the card that Gloria and Roy gave Jamie. He'd meant to slip it into his suitcase last night. Phyllis is making the face of someone who's just had a baby's dirty nappy thrust under her nose. On the front of the card is a picture of two cuddly teddy bears, both grey with blue noses, holding a Merry Christmas love heart between them. At least Gloria hadn't chosen a card with one blue bear and one pink bear. Now, Phyllis opens it up to read aloud the message inside. "*To Jamie and Billy. Hope you have a wonderful Christmas, love Mum and Dad.*" She turns to look at Jamie with bewilderment. He can see the idea congealing in her mind. She looks at Roy with raised eyebrows and a faint knowing smile. 'Funny sort of card to send two fellas.'

'Let me take your coat, Nan,' Jamie says, gently easing the card from her hands and setting it back on the mantelpiece. He thinks of something else to say. 'We should listen to the radio later. I want to see if the Spice Girls are at number one.'

'It's a bit early to start drinking, isn't it, Roy?' Phyllis says, surrendering to the question he asked moments ago, but keeping her eyes on Jamie, weighing him up. He can feel the pressure of an inquisition coming. She'll put him on the spot in front of everyone and watch him squirm. He knows it. But at this point, she just says, 'I'll have a whisky. With a drop of boiling water and half a spoon of sugar stirred in.' Then she throws her coat and scarf at Jamie. 'Here, pest. Take that.'

'On its way, Phyllis. Alf?' Roy says.

'Lager please, Roy.'

Roy gives Alf's coat to Jamie and disappears into the kitchen from where Jamie can hear the clattering of kitchen utensils and the ferocious slamming of doors and drawers.

'I hope you haven't squashed them presents,' Phyllis says.

Alf shakes his head and says, 'I can't hear what you're saying, Phyllis.' He adjusts his hearing-aid and turns sulkily to face the window.

Phyllis turns to Jamie. 'It's been one of those mornings. I've had a right game with him. One thing after another. He won't do as he's told. I told him to put his glasses in his jacket pocket and he didn't, so we had to go back for 'em. And just as we were leaving the house, he decides he needs the toilet. Well, that's an issue all in itself, isn't it? I had to get him back inside and upstairs and onto the khazi. And y'know how long it takes him, with his bleeding haemorrhoids and his bleeding moaning! 'I think I've strained meself,' he says. Oh and Jamie, the most graphic descriptions. He has to tell the precise colour and consistency and I say...'

'Don't go on, Phyllis,' Alf pleads, mysteriously regaining his hearing.

'...and his hands! That's another story. *Do you know,* he insists on washing his hands before *and* after using the toilet! He makes himself red raw. What's the doctor call it? Obsessive compulsive. That's it! Washes his back passage too. It's no wonder it's all dry and cracked. I've told him he's washing the natural oils out of his skin, but he knows best, doesn't he!' She prods Alf. 'If you want to end up with flesh like the arse end of a wind-burnt rhino, keep on. Just don't come crying to me for a jar of E45 when you're too sore to sit down… And of course, he marked his underwear, so now I'll have to do another boil wash.'

Alf turns and looks at Jamie. 'It's bloody Purgatory, I tell ya. She won't let up.'

Phyllis waves him away and calls to Roy in the kitchen, 'I can't wait to get my lips around that turkey.'

Taking that as his cue, Jamie dashes upstairs with the coats and looks at the bed—the bed where he was made. He begged and begged Gloria for a brother, but there was no chance. *You were too bloody painful.* Days after he'd been released into the world, Roy was up the clinic to have his tubes tied. And that was that.

He pulls his new phone from his pocket and types a message. *HOW R U?*

A response comes almost immediately. *HAVING LOVELY TIME. HOW R U?*

Jamie struggles to type a response with his thumb. *LIKE A FISH OUT OF WATER. MISSING U*, he replies, clicks send and puts the phone back in his pocket.

The bedroom is all chintz, lacy frills and plaster coving. There are doilies on top of doilies and collections of *stuff*, ornaments and photographs in frames, working-class proof that the Johnsons were here.

Jamie throws the coats on the bed. Then he has second thoughts. Phyllis will curse him if her gabardine gets creases in it. She likes it to be hung up. So he opens

Gloria's wardrobe to look for a hanger. It's crammed full of clothes. He has to push hard against the clump of dresses and blouses to retrieve one and something heavy falls out and hits him on the foot. He bends down to pick it up and feels the supple article in his hand—a heavy cylindrical handle with black leather bound all around it, ending in long strips of leather—a *cat-o-nine-tails* type of object, the likes of which he's only ever seen used to flog people in old oceanic costume dramas on the television. *Oh god!* Scenarios, involving his parents, flicker through his mind—he sees one end of the leather instrument in his mother's hand and with the quick movement of her arm, the leather straps of it lash his father's milky white bottom producing a cartoon yelp. Heart pounding, he thrusts the hanger and the leather object back in the wardrobe. He slams the door, throws Phyllis's coat on the bed and rubs his hands on his trousers.

He can hear raised voices as he runs back downstairs. Phyllis, holding a whisky, is looking daggers at Roy. Gloria is striding in from the kitchen, hair stuck to her face, now that she's grown it long, glasses steamed, pink Marigolds dripping. 'What do you mean, Roy? *We're not having turkey?*'

Gloria pushes her glasses back up her nose with her upper arm, avoiding suds from the rubber gloves that might spoil her lenses. 'Don't start Mother! You do this every year.'

107

'Look, don't upset yourself.' Roy tries to appease Phyllis.

'Be quiet a minute, Roy,' Gloria says. 'Why don't you choose another record or something?'

Phyllis's eyes burn into Gloria. She purses her pearlescent pink lips together in exaggerated indignation. 'Do *what* every year?'

'Complain. I could have put Beluga caviar and white truffles on the bloody table and you wouldn't be satisfied.'

'We always have turkey! It's *traditional.*' Phyllis's voice is barbed.

'Well, I decided to do pork this year. Something *different* for a change.' Gloria's eyes flick over at Jamie. 'If you don't like it, Roy can drive you back.'

Phyllis looks aghast. She throws back her whisky and scratches the back of her liver spotted hand.

'Doesn't seem much like Christmas without turkey, Gloria,' Alf says. 'Everyone has turkey at Christmas.'

Now she blasts her parents, the air a blur of her pink gloved fists and extended fingers. 'Well who ever said we all have to be like everyone else? I don't suppose Doris Day is sitting down to a turkey dinner right now.'

Jamie holds his breath as he waits for Gloria to trounce his grandmother's illusions about Doris Day and Rock Hudson.

'Oh, go on,' Phyllis rasps. 'Break my heart. Tell me why.' Her head is wobbling so that the neatly teased grey curls on her head quiver like the hair on a ferocious Bichon Frise.

'Because she's a bloody vegetarian,' Gloria says. 'Allegedly.'

Jamie battles with the image of his mother holding a whip in her hand, which is now contaminating his view of the situation. He pictures her wearing painfully high black stilettos and black high-necked all-in-one PVC body suit, the type he's only ever seen worn at clubs called *Thrash, Skin Tight, Rubber Masque, Torture Garden*.

He cuts in, 'Hey, Nan, your glass is empty,' and throws himself between them, trying to break the tension.

'I'll have an Advocaat this time,' Phyllis says, quickly.

Then Jamie turns to Gloria, nodding enthusiastically. 'It's after twelve you know, Mum, *you* could probably do with a drink as well.'

'You're bloody lucky that you get a Christmas at all,' Gloria continues rasping, even as he ushers her back into the kitchen. The sequins of her harlequin patterned Capri pants sparkling, despite the darkened atmosphere. 'You know, I do Christmas lunch *every* year and what thanks do I get?'

'Don't get yourself upset, Gloria,' Alf calls after them. 'Come on, why don't we open our presents?' Jamie can hear him rustling his carrier bags in the living room.

Gloria shouts, 'No. We'll do presents later, Dad. Your dinner's nearly ready.'

After Jamie returns with Phyllis's drink, they all sit smelling the food wafting in from the kitchen. Jamie is thrown a list of topics by Phyllis: *the cost of living in*

*London, work, friends* and, despite the fact that she saw the card on the mantelpiece, *is he courting?* Every time Billy's name or their life in London are mentioned Jamie jumps out of his seat and refills the glasses until Gloria finally calls them all into the dining room.

She's dishing up an enormous feast of delicious Christmas grub minus the turkey. Having removed her apron and glasses, she is now the picture of glamour. Roy carves the joint and Gloria serves vegetables. Alf is hunched over his plate, salivating. Phyllis is tight-lipped, eyeing the joint of pork as if she wants to wrestle it to the ground.

'Roasters, Dad?' Gloria asks, holding a dish next to his plate.

'Yes,' Alf replies, smacking his lips together like a hungry dog. 'Your roasters are the best I've ever tasted, all fluffed up at the edges.'

Jamie wonders at Alf's appetite; even with his grumbling appendix and his piles, his plate is piled high with vegetables.

'There's plenty left, Dad. You can come back for more later.'

'Go on, save yourself the journey, Glo. Put a few more on there. I'm famished.' Being of the Protect and Survive generation, he places his arms on either side of his plate as if worried someone might swipe his roast potatoes. He would always put four boxes of teabags into the shopping trolley, four bags of rice, four tins of beans, four of everything. Hoarding, just in case nuclear war broke out.

Phyllis is surrounded by drink, unable, as ever, to turn it away. She has a cup of coffee, into which she's poured the remaining Advocaat, joined by yet another whisky, a large glass of bubbly and a red wine. Jamie is surprised to see she hasn't brought her usual bottle of Lambrusco.

His mobile phone buzzes in his pocket. Another text. *I LOVE U,* Billy says. Jamie thinks about Billy having Christmas lunch with his own family.

*HOW MUCH?* he replies.

'What's that, our Jamie?' Phyllis asks, pointing to the phone.

Before he can reply, Gloria calls over, 'They've all got them these days. Mobile phones are the new craze.'

Billy's response comes back. *4 BAGS OF SUGAR, 2 PINTS OF MILK & A PKT OF CHEESE & ONION CRISPS.* Jamie smiles.

'Put it away now,' Gloria says. 'Not at the dinner table.'

Alf is tucking into his dinner already. 'Wait 'til Mum is sitting,' Jamie says. 'She's the one who cooked it.'

'You won't change him, Jamie,' Phyllis says, picking one glass up and putting another empty one down. 'He's got the manners of a pig.' Then she looks at Alf. 'Couldn't you get any more on the plate?'

'You enjoy your dinner, Dad,' Gloria says lovingly. 'Don't you worry about me.' Jamie frowns at her but she shakes her head. 'At least he's not causing trouble while he's got his head in the nose bag.'

Jamie watches the gravy dangling from Alf's four-day old facial hair. He can't help but smile. 'Couldn't afford a razor today, Grandad?' He hands him a napkin and points to his top lip.

'Thanks,' Alf grumbles and wipes his mouth. Gloria and Roy join them to eat. Gloria makes them all put party hats on. 'It's traditional,' she says, pointedly, pulling one over Grandad's sweaty forehead. 'Right, I want everyone to have a nice time. Tuck in.'

'Raise your glasses. Raise your glasses,' Phyllis says. She rearranges the selection of drinks in front of her and finally goes for the red wine. They all cheer, 'Merry Christmas,' and clink their glasses together.

Then there is a hush—just the sound of them chewing loudly and Alf scraping his cutlery on the side of his plate. Phyllis is enthusiastically biting down on a piece of crackling. Obviously, she is enjoying it so much that she's forgotten the missing turkey.

Then Alf nudges her: 'Pull a cracker with me, Phyllis.' They pull the cracker with a grand commotion, both cheering like school children. Glasses and cutlery shake as Alf unwraps a pirate's eye patch and puts it on. Then he puckers his drooling lips at Phyllis. 'Give us a kiss,' he says, and they start canoodling.

'Don't be disgusting,' Jamie laughs. 'We're eating!'

'Jamie, lighten up,' Gloria says. 'Nice to see they're still in love at their age.'

Phyllis pulls away. 'Stop it, Alf. You're upsetting Jamie.' She takes another slug of wine.

'I just don't like all this fruitiness at the table.' Jamie says.

Everyone joins in the laughter. 'I'm sorry, old *fruit*,' Phyllis says and winks. Jamie enjoys her casual use of the word *fruit* and wonders if she knows it derives from ancient gay slang. 'Billy at his Mum's today?' she asks. He can feel that she is working up to a question—some uncomfortable query—to put him on the spot.

Alf says. 'It's only because I love her.' He looks at Roy. 'Can't keep me bloody hands off her.'

'Oh, aye?' Roy says, nodding at him, encouragingly.

Alf turns to Phyllis who is now pushing a roast potato around her plate with a fork. She has begun to look a little pale.

'Is that right, Phyllis?' Roy asks. 'Does he give you hot loving?'

Gloria bursts out laughing hysterically. 'Roy, stop it. That's my mother you're talking to. She doesn't need any encouragement.'

'If I could have my time again,' Alf says. 'I'd show her.'

Jamie can see Phyllis rising to the occasion, doubling in size like an angry wildcat, hair standing on end. She places down her knife and fork, cleanly on the tablecloth, and takes a quick swig of red wine, leaving greasy lipstick on the glass. Her lips are pursed, creating vertical wrinkles under her nose. '*He* don't give me hot love anymore! You must be bloody joking. He can't. That *thing* went cold years ago.' She wiggles her little finger in the air. That should be enough but, no, she goes on. 'It's bloody useless. Shrivelled up and no bigger than the end of my finger. I don't know what he thinks he can do with it. He can't even piss through it properly. Do you know, our toilet-bowl has got to be fifteen inches or more in diameter and he can't hit the middle of it. The bleeding bathroom carpet stinks of stale piss.'

'Mother, that's enough!' Gloria growls, showing her teeth.

Jamie's cheeks are hot. Roy is hiding behind his wine glass. Jamie looks at Alf fiddling uncomfortably with his hearing-aid again and looking down into his dinner. He looks destroyed. His watery lower eyelids are wetter and more bloodshot than usual.

'Hot love? You must be joking.'

'Mother!' Gloria shouts this time. Her hand comes down hard on the table making everyone's cutlery rattle against the plates. Alf spills his wine.

'Now, look what you've gone and done, ya bloody silly oaf,' Phyllis says.

'Enough!' Gloria snaps. 'I swear to God, Mother, if you spoil another Christmas... Just eat your bloody dinner and shut up.'

They eat in silence while Gloria mops up the wine. After they have finished, without a word, she clears all the plates away. Roy moves to get up. 'Let me help you?'

'No. Just let me do it.' She shows him the palm of her hand. In Jamie's mind, she's in black PVC again, holding a leather paddle—only this time the PVC suit has morphed into an image Gloria and Jamie had once seen of the renowned performance artist, Leigh Bowery, in the arts supplement of a Sunday newspaper. And he wonders, after all, if they really are as different as he'd first thought. Gloria blows out. 'I'm fine. Just leave me. I'm fine.'

Roy settles back into his seat. They all sit obediently as she collects the cutlery and replaces the spit-sodden serviettes with crisp clean ones. She moves methodically around the table, removing the gravy boat, the remaining meat from the joint and the vegetable dishes.

Jamie risks rising to help her load the dishwasher. Gloria, rigid with anger, quickly brings her hand up to her mouth to stifle a sob. Then she's crying on his shoulder. Phyllis rushes past. 'Oh God! I think I'm going to be sick.' They all look at her dashing out of the room, clasping a napkin to her mouth.

Gloria is shaking her head, wiping tears away with a tissue. Her lips are stretched across clenched teeth. 'Roy, how much has she had to drink?'

Roy closes his eyes at the sound of Phyllis retching into the toilet bowl. 'Jesus,' he says, 'I've only just decorated that bathroom.' They've had it done modern. Plush white, no fuss. Gloria places dessert-spoons, bowls and a jug of single cream on the table. She goes to the fridge. Alf watches attentively. She's returning with dessert as Phyllis shuffles back into the room, wiping her face with toilet tissue, her mouth a gash of smudged lipstick.

'That really was a lovely bit of pork, our Gloria,' she says, though she's looking directly at Jamie.

Oh no. She's got that look on her face. Maybe it's his turn to visit the toilet.

'So, our Jamie...' she begins.

Jamie can feel his neck getting warm and redness in his cheeks.

'...when you buy this flat—what colour are you and Billy going to paint the bedroom?'

'Hot pink!' he jests, and everyone laughs, including Alf, despite his selective hearing.

The phone buzzes in his pocket again. He looks at it. *U WILL B SWIMMING IN THE SEA AGAIN SOON. FOUND ANY COMMON GROUND?* Billy asks.

*MORE THAN I'D LIKE TO ADMIT,* Jamie types back, clicks send and then wonders to himself if it might be nice to stay a little longer than he'd planned.

'Right,' Gloria says sharply, taking a deep breath. Alf, Roy and Phyllis all stop to look at her. In her hands she's holding a glass vessel layered with broad stripes of white, pink, yellow and deep red at the bottom.

'Who's for trifle?' she says, jubilantly.

Phyllis's mouth drops open. 'But what about the Christmas pudding?'

# Two Little Ducks

'Six and nine, sixty-nine... Two fat ladies, eighty-eight.' The bingo caller, brushed with glamour—rhinestone jacket, black quiff, solarium tan—stares over his booth—a moist grin, white teeth, something obscene in his eyes.

Mid-game, Billy weaves through grey air saturated with fag smoke, down the gangway of old ladies. Phyllis sits at a table with her entourage, stabbing their sheets of bingo numbers with inky dabbers. 'Here he is,' she says in between numbers and indicates the space she's kept for him. 'Put y'bum down there.' Billy places drinks down for Phyllis and her friends and slides into the seat, where her newspaper is open at the classifieds. 'Pass me that dabber, Ivy. This one's dead.' Phyllis presses a finger to her lips, ensuring silence, until somebody shrieks an orgasmic—

'Here y'are!' and the caller confirms the winner's numbers.

'Can I speak now?'

'That's it,' Phyllis says, taking the last drag on a cigarette so carefully smoked, at least an inch of unbroken ash remains attached. 'I won't be going to the Bahamas this week.' She leans over and kisses Billy. 'No Jamie?'

'Nah, not tonight... he's working on an assignment,' he says, pushing a whiskey and soda towards Ivy Warner, Phyllis's bingo partner. 'So he's sent me instead.' The bingo caller steps down from his podium as music begins to play—*A Design for Life* by the *Manic Street Preachers*.

'You didn't have to come out alone on my account.'

121

'A night out with my Phyllis? Wouldn't miss it for the world.' His eyes track rhinestone jacket and black quiff from the caller's booth, past the tables until he reaches the bar.

'You know, Jamie's been coming to the bingo with me since he was knee-high,' Phyllis says.

'Shouldn't you be here *together*?' Ivy says, from across the table. 'Last night before you head back to London?'

'Where's *Mr* Warner?' Phyllis spits, then looks back at Billy. 'Remember last time? You and Jamie won all that money—enough for a weekend in Amsterdam.'

'It won't last,' Ivy says, scratching the back of her hand lined with raised blue veins.

'You can't say that, Ivy,' Billy says. 'We're a proper couple. Just like you and Mr Warner.' Billy breathes out and lets his eyes fall onto the newspaper classifieds. *An Oasis of Pleasure in a Hectic World. Glasshouse Health Spa. Looking for escape? Open 365 days a year.*

'I expect we're not enough for Jamie.' Ivy's lighting up now. The fringe of her long platinum-grey hair is browned from nicotine. 'Ideas above his station, that one—now that he's living the high-life in London.'

Billy half-laughs. 'Hardly, Ivy. He lives in a box room in student digs.'

Ivy tears up her bingo tickets and throws them into the centre of the table. 'Yes, and when he does hit the big time, he won't remember us.'

Phyllis throws her dabber at Ivy. 'That's my grandson you're talking about.'

'He won't forget you, Ivy,' Billy says, gently. 'He just wants different things out of life, and round here, you know—'

'Round here, what?' Ivy asks.

Scanning the room of drinkers, glass collectors, men playing a game of darts in the corner—Billy's eyes pause on a poster near the bar. *Welston Constitutional Club. Mon— Quiz Night (Chicken in a Basket), Tues—Bingo, Wed— Karaoke, Thurs—The Gone Wrong Sisters Drag Show, Fri— Disco, Sat—Country and Western Night, Sun—Shanice.*

'Mr Warner can't control himself anymore,' Phyllis says. 'He's having a bag fitted.'

Billy sighs. 'Where you are born and who you are shouldn't exclude you from anything, whatsoever.'

'Don't get deep, Billy,' Phyllis says. 'You'll lose her completely.'

'What you talking about my husband for?' Ivy says in disgust and then turns back to Billy. 'Jamie's not excluded. If he'd learnt a trade like his father, he'd have a bloody good business in roofing.'

'Yes, I expect that would be true, Ivy, if he'd wanted to do that. He'd have a very strong network. But the thing is—'

'We're all looking for something to carry us away from the mundane,' Phyllis says, 'while we're crawling our way across the globe… even you, Ivy. Don't deny it.' Phyllis lights up another cigarette. 'She doesn't like to brag about it but our Ivy used to work in Soho. A rather well-kept secret, Billy—our Ivy here used to answer the telephone in a—'

'A madam?' Billy says.

'It wasn't like that,' Ivy says.

Phyllis mimes a telephone with her left hand and mimics madam Ivy. 'Hello. House of Sin. How may I help you? Oh, yes I'm sure that can be arranged. It's sixty for a half hour or a hundred for the full service. All tastes catered for.'

Ivy looks a bit wounded. 'It was a change of scenery.'

'Exactly!' Phyllis says. 'Nothing so edgy round here, is there? You should be with your own kind, Billy. Not sitting here with the old women.'

§

Billy steps from his car and walks with nervous excitement towards the innocuous doorway, pausing as he waits to be buzzed in. He'd never do this with Jamie. He'd never understand. Too vanilla. The door opens and he's in. He hands over his money at the reception desk to a bald man, attractive—perhaps once handsome. He collects a towel and walks through into the busy locker room—smelling of men and chlorine.

It's almost the same as going to the swimming baths.

Undressed, naked—wearing just a towel, vulnerable, Billy pads round—a sauna, steam room, cinema, swimming pool with Grecian ornaments that remind him of Gloria's living room and prompt a wave of guilt. Beyond is a darkened sex maze only dimly lit with red light.

He decides to visit the bar for a drink before setting out on adventure. A beer. The man on the stool next to him drinks whiskey and soda. The barman flounces up and down in flip-flops. Scanning the many men perched on barstools, wearing just towels—Billy's eyes pause on a poster on the wall. *The Glasshouse Gentlemen's Health Spa. Mon—Sports Day, Tues—Bears, Wed—Underwear, Thurs—Leather, Fri—Disco, Sat—Cruise, Sun—Cruise.*

'First time, honey?' the barman asks.

'Does it show?' Billy says.

'You're safe, darling. We're all friends here. Go on. Go get 'em, tiger.'

He finishes his drink and goes on the prowl. All he can hear are the fetid whispers of strangers in the dark, the sounds of heavy breathing and of bare feet on the sticky floor.

'Fancy a threesome?' a disembodied voice asks in the darkness. It unnerves him. Billy weaves through air saturated with amyl-nitrate, down the maze of corridors. Only a few narrow shafts of red light filter through the gaps between the door and the doorframes of the cubicles where men collect for sex. The floor is peppered with sachets of lube and empty condom wrappers. Along the corridor twenty or more figures can be seen leaning, prowling. Silence, but for the grunts, snorts and spits of men shuffling around in the dark and the groan of an occasional orgasm.

Billy stops. He has his eye on a man who has come to stand just next to him—rugged, tanned, short neatly trimmed stubble, black hair sculpted into a shiny quiff. In the half-light he gives the impression of being shy but Billy can see he knows exactly what he's doing. There are a couple of men opposite, passing a small bottle back and forth, and holding it to their nostrils.

Sweaty palms.

Tingly neck.

The tanned guy rubs his chest and fingers his left nipple. He leans closer to Billy then steps backwards into one of the empty cubicles, his silhouette now defined by the red glow from inside. Billy edges forward. He's trembling, adrenaline coursing through his veins. His hands go up in front of him, tentatively feeling his way through the darkness. On the threshold, he knows. This is him. This is part of who he is.

Inside, there's a padded leather bench, just long enough to lie down on. The glow of red is brighter in here and it's possible to see the man's smile. They lock the door behind them.

'What's your name?' the man whispers. He finds the man's voice a little disturbing. Billy hasn't come here to make conversation.

'Billy,' he says, not encouraging anything further.

'I'm Russell.' He feels the man's hand stroke his nipple and ruffle his chest hair. 'Been here long?'

They kiss for a moment. 'Long enough to have a scout around.'

'I just arrived from work,' the man whispers.

'What do you do?' Billy asks, instantly wishing he hadn't.

The man's hands go to Billy's now flaccid penis and says, 'I'm a bingo caller.'

# Proceed
# Undeterred

Jamie stares out of his grandmother's kitchen window at the sunlight bleaching her neighbours' houses and feels his heart sag. He misses London already—it was all over so quickly. Barely had a chance to get to know the place. Some of his fellow students were able to stay on after their degrees, but they had fallen straight into highly paid jobs or had trust funds.

Jamie is a toned-down version of himself for Welston. Best to not draw too much attention. If he makes it back, he can wear whatever he chooses—sequins and glitter. He'll get cabs everywhere. Famous people will stop and chat to him in the street. He will be friends with all the right people. He'll spend his time with artists and drag queens and handsome men in leather jackets. And unicorns. One day, there will be a red carpet, upon which he will be wearing an electric blue Tom Ford suit, walking an adorable blue-eyed Russian husky puppy, flanked by Holly Johnson and Boy George. The moment will be frozen in a burst of camera flashes.

'Jamie, they'll eat you alive down there,' Gloria says, almost gleefully.

The rainbow film of Jamie's soapy reverie ruptures as he finishes washing the last saucepan and pulls the plug in the sink; reality feels grey again.

'Leave him alone, Gloria,' Sandra interrupts, pouring four cups of tea but spilling most of it onto Phyllis' kitchen table.

The three women and Jamie form corners of a small square within the lilac-painted room, facing each other for the weekly family brew. Phyllis is standing—multitasking while the others are seated. Jamie has his legs up on a chair.

'London's not for people like us,' Gloria continues. 'Why don't you find a job around here, where you belong?' She looks at Phyllis. 'Mother, talk some sense into the boy, will you?'

'Don't rope me into your arguments, Gloria,' Phyllis says, heaving laundry from one side of an antiquated twin-tub to the other with a pair of wooden tongs. She holds aloft a pair of Alf's dripping white y-fronts, checking the crotch for remaining soil marks. Gloria and Sandra tried to bully Nan into upgrading to a front-loader but she wouldn't have any of it. Why get rid of a perfectly good washing machine? It still does the job. Jamie has seen her sneer at them, calling them the *wasteful generation*.

'I've got enough on my plate with *him* in there. He's sat on that toilet four times already this morning! *Me?* I go once a day and that's it: clean as a whistle. I never wake up in the night needing to go, either. *Him*, he's fixated with the bloody toilet.'

All this kind of talk makes Jamie's stomach turn over.

'Think of the expense, Jamie.' Gloria says. 'You'll be working all hours just to keep a roof over your head. There won't be any social life, if that's what you're imagining.

And then there's the distance.'

'Mum, it's London, not *Mars*. And I've been there three years already! I know what to expect. And Billy is still there!'

Jamie closes his eyes. Thing is, Mum is right. London *is* expensive. He hasn't even got the deposit and month's advance rent that is practically unavoidable in the capital.

'And for how long do you think he's going to last down there, painting pictures? Listen to reason, Jamie,' Gloria says. 'Studying is one thing. Living there full-time is another. You've *not* thought this through. Hey—where are you off to?'

Jamie is already leaving the room. 'I'm going to sit on that toilet that you never stop bloody talking about.' On the stairs he passes Alf, wearing a tea-stained singlet and jogging bottoms. He's carrying a bag of prunes.

At the top of the stairs, Jamie hears Phyllis berate Gloria: 'Always meddlin', always sticking your great beak in. Why can't you leave the boy be?'

As soon as Jamie's arse cheeks touch the cold toilet seat, the seat in the tiny bathroom where he's sought sanctuary so many other times, he's reminded of all the other toilets in which he's hidden, sitting staring at the same spot on the floor, regardless of location—the orange and red geometric patterns of his nan's bathroom carpet, swirling and making his eyes go whizzy, the beige plush of his mother's bathroom pedestal mat, or the grimy

133

tiling of municipal toilets, ammonia battling the putrid smell of excrement. Sitting there has always been a kind of meditation. In the toilet, he could lock the world out. Anything difficult—an awkward question, an argument, an unwanted knock at the front door—the toilet is where he would find himself, like a cat crouched in terror beneath the safety of a stout chair.

His bowels groan, and as they relax a memory comes to him. It was years ago now, but Jamie experiences it with painful clarity, as if it was happening again. He hears raised voices downstairs, voices from the past. His mother crying; Phyllis's voice, consoling:

'What's happened now, Gloria? Come on.'

Gloria sobs again. 'Mother, I think our Jamie is being bullied at school.'

'But they've just broken up for the summer. It'll be secondary school for him in September. And he's always happy when he comes here.'

And then Alf: 'Well, what do you expect when he walks around like a little wench?'

Jamie can remember hearing him, word for word. Even now it makes his eyes water. 'Knitting! In the school holidays! When I was a boy, you couldn't keep me in. You've let him spend too much time with the women. Why not put him in a pinny and have done with it? If you ask me—'

'No-one *was* asking you, Alf,' Phyllis had said in response.

'You should have sent him to Boy's Brigade,' Alf went on. 'That would have knocked some character into—'

'Will you shut up!' Phyllis interrupted. 'Go up the garden and cut me a cabbage. I've got a piece of belly draft for your dinner. Unless you'd prefer to go without? You could do with losing some weight off that fat arse of yours.'

Jamie had thought he was past all this, but the memories are still potent. Why does he do this—open old wounds? They *had* eventually sent him to Boys Brigade. There, he learnt the Lord's Prayer and was expected to repeat it out loud each week. There was also marching and stamping of feet and standing to attention. And ironically, he got to do a lot of needlecraft—one of those things Grandad Alf called *women's work*. Jamie had never understood that. What difference did it make if he was a boy or a girl? He was better at it than all the other boys, thanks to Nan's teaching. He received regular compliments on his blanket stitch, on his chain stitch and his French knots. But it hadn't been the Boys Brigade or Grandad Alf's snide remarks that got to him that summer.

He distinctly remembers leaving Nan's house that day, after overhearing his mother crying—he and Gloria turning at the corner, as was tradition, to wave to Nan standing on her doorstep, Phyllis waving back as if they were sailing away on a liner that would take months to return and then, halfway home, passing his best friend's house.

'I haven't heard you mention Stephen for a while,' Gloria said in a voice that stretched beyond general inquisitiveness. 'Why doesn't he call round anymore?'

Jamie shrugged. 'He's busy, I suppose.'

'I thought you'd be spending more time with each other over summer?'

Jamie shrugged again, focussing on a bit of chewing gum stuck to the pavement.

'Jamie,' Gloria said, softly. 'You know, secrets are better when shared.'

'I don't have any secrets.'

'Well, at least you'll see Stephen when you start back. Nice to have a familiar face at the new school.'

Jamie felt his eyes stinging. He couldn't explain that Stephen had started to taunt him, taking the side of the other boys. The *mean* boys.

'Mum, can I have some money to go to the video shop? There's a new movie I want to watch.'

'You can come to the wool shop with me, if you're at a loose end.'

'I'd rather stay at home.' Maybe Grandad Alf was right about the knitting, after all.

'You must have watched every film in the shop at least twice. Why aren't you out seeing your friends?'

Jamie stayed silent. He hated being alone. But no matter how he tried to conform, he was never accepted.

'You should enjoy the summers while you still have

them.' Gloria smiled sadly before giving him five pounds from her purse. 'When you're older, you won't ever get this time back.'

But Jamie knew that he wouldn't ever want it back. He still remembers the look on her face: she pitied him. He tries to shake the image from his mind. Why is it always the same memories that come back? The same stories that he keeps telling himself. Even after so long. Is this really who he is? He feels his stomach groan again. He must have been sat up here for ten minutes at least. He wonders if Nan has finished the washing yet, or if they've changed the bleeding subject now, or if Grandad has actually gone to get that cabbage.

Gloria had told him to choose two films. 'Something we can all watch together after tea.' She'd put her purse away and smiled again. This time more encouragingly.

Shortly after that, he was taking a short cut through the housing estate to the video rental shop, dawdling past the old chapel, and the graveyard with its huge wrought iron fence, then across wasteland littered with rusty mattress springs and scattered pornographic magazines—mainly women in uncomfortable poses, pretending to enjoy being used by men. Then a short cut past abandoned garages with drab, rusty doors, the floor strewn with broken beer bottles, abandoned hub caps and discarded condoms.

And that was when he saw it, sprayed in red paint on a pale blue garage door, like dried blood on the walls of a morgue.

*Jamie Johnson is a Nancy Boy.*

He never went that way to the video shop again.

That summer was the longest and loneliest in his life—far, friendless bike rides, sitting at home watching movies in the dark, endless wandering around cemeteries. The dead were friendlier than the living.

And in September, at his new school, although he made friends to sit with during lessons, breaks and lunchtimes were too often fearful. He was picked on and taunted by other pupils—always boys, always the same boys—with Stephen who used to be his friend among them.

*Bumboy, gaylord, poofter, Nancy. 'Don't touch him; he's got AIDS.'*

They mocked him with vile words, or hurt him with fists and feet. They humiliated him, spitting on him, or damaging his property, ripping his clothes or dragging him through mud, so that when he got home to his mother, he would have to invent some elaborate story to explain away his appearance, to throw her off the scent.

He could tell her anything but the truth. How could he bear the shame? What if she found out? They would disown him, throw him out. There was no way he could talk to his teachers about it and there was no one else like him to turn to. He knew what he was, but he couldn't bring himself to fully admit it—not even to himself. He'd seen what happened to other people, on television and in the newspapers.

# I'D SHOOT MY SON IF HE HAD AIDS, SAYS VICAR!

# BRITAIN THREATENED BY GAY VIRUS PLAGUE!

## SCRAP EASTENDERS CALL OVER GAY KISS

For Jamie, nowhere felt safe. There was a period when he was so sad—no one used words like *depression* or *mental health* back then—he would fake illness to avoid school. This made him even sadder because he enjoyed learning. He spent days in bed because, as Gloria liked to remind him, 'If you're well enough to get out of bed, you're well enough to go to school.'

Led by whatever he read in the redtops that landed every morning on their doormat and cranky from endless nightshifts, Roy hadn't always been the amenable, tolerant man that he is now. One time, Jamie overheard him snapping at Gloria; the words hooked into Jamie and never let him go:

'You insisted on doing things your way. Look how that's turned out. The little fairy can't stand up for himself. I should have straightened him out years ago. I should have taken my belt off to him when he was a—'

'Roy Johnson, if you ever lay a finger on my boy, I swear, I'll dissolve you in acid and bury the remains under that patio. Mark my words.'

Jamie's father had changed his opinions with the times. And eventually Jamie's mother didn't believe her son's stories anymore and could no longer lie to herself about the bullying; she marched Jamie into school for a confrontation. The head of year thanked Gloria for bringing the issue to her attention. She assured them that steps would be taken, the situation closely monitored. But those were just words.

No one ever talked about *why* Jamie was being bullied. Gloria didn't ask the school and they didn't tell—not even when Jamie had lost so much weight that he had to punch new holes in his belt to keep his trousers up, not when his lunch was stolen so that he had nothing to eat—not that he ever felt like eating much—not even when Jamie's shoes were wrenched from his feet and thrown into the school pond. No one asked Jamie any questions at all. If they had, what would he have said? The truth? He couldn't trust his teachers to protect him. He couldn't tell his parents. He already knew what his father thought of him.

Then one day, walking home, Jamie's tormentors caught up.

'Here he is, the fucking weirdo!'

'Fucking AIDS spreader,' another yelled.

One of them shoved Jamie in the back.

'Why don't you leave me alone?' Jamie asked. He tried not to engage with them, tried not to make eye contact.

'Tried to get us suspended, didn't you?' one of them spat.

'You'll never turn the teachers against us. They can see you for the dirty little faggot that you are.'

Jamie ran then, sprinting into the wooded wasteland, halfway between home and school, that everyone called *The Burn*. He ran as fast as he could, tears blurring his vision, but he could hear their feet thumping along behind him.

Then something hard and sharp hit his head and all at once he was on the floor, one of the boys on top of him. Jamie could hear himself screaming. He tried to escape but everything felt as if it were moving with the reluctance of a toilet cistern refilling.

The boy had a rock in his hands, lifted high above his head.

Jamie could see it coming down, coming down at his face.

With strength he never knew he had in him, he wrenched himself half-free, just before the rock caught him between the eyes.

There was a moment of shock; then the realisation hit him: the boy had deliberately tried to smash his skull. With that came a surge of adrenalin; he ran and ran and *ran*.

Across the wasteland he went, through the housing estate, along the disused railway, until he reached the steps leading to his street. Halfway down them he felt a sudden looseness in his gut.

His bowels—he couldn't control himself.

141

Reaching towards his arse, he tried pressing the seat of his trousers to his backside, in the vain hope of plugging the hole. But he couldn't stop the sudden evacuation. A foul stench hit him and he felt liquid shit dribbling down the inside of his trousers. He clenched his arse cheeks, trying to stem the flow but it just kept oozing.

'Please, *no.*'

Finally, at the bottom of the steps, he broke into a sort of run-cum-canter, hoping that he could reach home before the shit reached his shoes. Hot tears made his cheeks sore. His head swivelled side to side like a surveillance camera. *Please, nobody notice*; he couldn't bear anyone seeing him like this. He was half running, half walking now, trying to hold the rest of it in. Rounding the bend to the cul-de-sac where he lived, he made a dash for home, pulling his front door keys from his pocket. He was thinking about getting the key into the keyhole before he even reached the front garden; he aimed carefully. There! He pushed it in on the first attempt and he turned it in the lock. The door opened.

Dropping his bag, he leapt up the stairs to the bathroom, a revolting belch of gas escaping his arsehole as he went. He hurdled into the bath itself, pulling off his clothes.

Everything started to go grey and for a moment he felt as if he might pass out. His school jumper was only halfway over his head when he realised, he couldn't hold the rest of it in any longer; an abrupt effluence of brown sludge emptied into the bath, the dam burst at last.

It was all over him, his legs and feet covered with shit. His underpants, still wrapped around his ankles, were sodden with brown slime.

He was obscene.

This was what *they* had made of him: a body of excrement, excrement to be flushed away.

And then over the noise of his shaky, ragged breathing, he heard something that might have been the rattle of the key in the front door downstairs.

*His mother?*

The thought galvanised him.

She mustn't see this. No mother should ever see her son like—

Jamie tried wiping the disgusting fluid from his legs but that only made things worse. Now it was all over his hands. He reached for the shower head thinking he could wash it away, but it slipped through his fingers. Panicking, he turned on the bath taps, but that proved a big mistake— the water pressure.

Brown liquid blasted everywhere.

Shit on the carpet.

Shit on the shower curtain.

Shit and undigested food in the plughole.

143

Then his mother's voice—right outside the bathroom:
'Bloody Nora! What on earth is that smell?'

The door handle started to turn. In haste and covered in shit, he hadn't locked the door.

'No! Mum, don't—!'

But of course, Gloria didn't listen.

'Oh my God!' she screamed. 'What's happened?'

§

Gloria's shrill voice echoes in Nan's hallway from the foot of the stairs: 'Are you alright up there, Jamie?'

'Jesus!' he shouts back. 'I'm fine! Can't I even have a dump in private?'

He wipes, flushes before going to stand at the sink. Massaging soap into his hands, he works up a lather; he coats the backs of his hands and rubs it expertly around the webbed skin between each finger. Then he links his fingers, making sure the soap gets under his fingernails. While abluting, he stares at the blur of trees and houses and gardens—coloured shapes behind the frosted bathroom window—like a partially developed photograph, an image not yet clarified.

He thinks of London. His student life there had been a rehearsal, nothing more. He'd had no money; he hadn't explored.

What holds him back now, he wonders.

He thinks about what he has learned on his degree. How to compose a picture. How to reframe it to tell a different story.

London is an unopened gift—what could lie inside its wrapping?

Mum is right, it's expensive. But there is work there, more than there is in Welston. It isn't only an expense, but an opportunity.

The bars, the clubs, the stars, the *art*.

And the people—people who don't find his existence abhorrent…

And Billy. He misses Billy who will be starting the last year of his fine art degree.

Beyond this blurred window, beyond Welston, is the possibility of transformation.

When he gets back downstairs, they all—Phyllis, Sandra, Alf but not Gloria—cheer as if he's just returned from a long voyage. Gloria looks as if she's been crying again.

Sandra says, 'We were going to send out a search party.'

Phyllis says, 'You haven't got the jollop, have you? I hope you haven't made a mess up there!'

'No,' Jamie says. He places a hand on his stomach, relieved that it is settling. 'I've been thinking.'

'Oh yes,' Phyllis replies. 'On the karzi?'

'That's where *I* do all my best thinking,' Alf says.

Sandra has a questioning look on her face, as if she's

waiting for him to make an announcement.

Jamie smiles at his mother, who has tried so long to shelter him in the best way she can. He hopes she will understand.

'I've come to a decision.'

Acknowledgements

A version of *Tales of the Suburbs* was published within my collection of 'working-class' fiction, *He's Done Ever So Well for Himself.*

Deepest gratitude to my mum, my dad and the wonderful people of the West Midlands, who inspired the characters in this book.

Thank you to the following for their invaluable feedback while readying this book for publication:
Philip Ridley, Nathan Evans, Kit de Waal, Alex Hopkins, James Maker, Joshua Davis, Bartholomew Bennett and Jake Jones.

Thanks to Joe Mateo for his gorgeous cover design and to Bartholomew Bennett for his forensic eyes.

Thanks to our publising assistant, Petronella Carter, and our digital marketing guru, Sam Missingham.

Very special thanks to Benedicta Norell for her generous patronage which has helped to bring this book into being. And to Anthony Psaila, who let me stay in his flat in Margate so that I could finish writing this by the sea.

Lastly, thanks to everyone who keeps buying and reading the books.

My loyal following—I love you.

# Also from Inkandescent

# *Kissing the Lizard*

by Justin David

**Part Two of the Welston World Sagas**
*In the desert, no one can hear you, queen*

Justin David's newly-released novella is part creepy coming-of-age story, part black-comedy, set partly in buzzing 1990s London and partly in barren New Mexico wildlands.

When Jamie meets Matthew in Soho, he's drawn to his new-age charms. But when he follows his new friend across the planet to a remote earth-ship in Taos, bizarre incidents begin unfolding and Matthew's real nature reveals itself: he's a manipulative monster at the centre of a strange cult. Jamie finds himself at the centre a disturbing psychological nightmare as they seize the opportunity to recruit a new member. Pushed to his limits, lost in a shifting sagebrush landscape, can Jamie trust anyone to help him? And will he ever see home again?

This evocatively set desert gothic expertly walks the line between macabre humour and terrifying tension.

*'There's not much rarer than a working class voice in fiction, except maybe a gay working class voice. We need writers like Justin David.'*
PAUL McVEIGH, author of *The Good Son*

# Also from Inkandescent

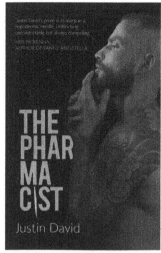

## THE PHARMACIST
by Justin David

### Part Three of the Welston World Sagas
*when love is the drug*

Twenty-four-year-old Billy is beautiful and sexy. Albert—The Pharmacist—is a compelling but damaged older man, and a veteran of London's late '90s club scene. After a chance meeting in the heart of the London's East End, Billy is seduced into the sphere of Albert. An unconventional friendship develops, fuelled by Albert's queer narratives and an endless supply of narcotics. Alive with the twilight times between day and night, consciousness and unconsciousness, the foundations of Billy's life begin to irrevocably shift and crack, as he fast-tracks toward manhood. This story of lust, love and loss is homoerotic bildungsroman at its finest.

*'At the heart of David's The Pharmacist is an oddly touching and bizarre love story, a modern day Harold and Maude set in the drugged-up world of pre-gentrification Shoreditch. The dialogue, especially, bristles with glorious life.'*
JONATHAN KEMP

*'As lubricious as early Alan Hollinghurst,*
*The Pharmacist is a welcome reissue from Inkandescent, and the perfect introduction to a singular voice in gay literature.'*
THE TIMES LITERARY SUPPLEMENT

# Also from Inkandescent

## THREADS
### by Nathan Evans & Justin David

If Alice landed in London not Wonderland this book might be the result. Threads is the first collection from Nathan Evans, each poem complemented by a bespoke photograph from Justin David and, like Tenniel's illustrations for Carroll, picture and word weft and warp to create an alchemic (rabbit) whole.

On one page, the image of an alien costume, hanging surreally beside a school uniform on a washing line, accompanies a poem about fleeing suburbia. On another, a poem about seeking asylum accompanies the image of another displaced alien on an urban train. Spun from heartfelt emotion and embroidered with humour, Threads will leave you aching with longing and laughter.

*'In this bright and beautiful collaboration, poetry and photography join hands, creating sharp new ways to picture our lives and loves.'*
NEIL BARTLETT

*'Two boldly transgressive poetic voices'*
MARISA CARNESKY

# Also from Inkandescent

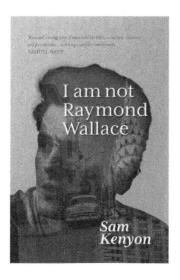

## I am not Raymond Wallace
### by Sam Kenyon

Manhattan, 1963: weeks before the assassination of President Kennedy, fresh-faced Raymond Wallace lands in the New York Times newsroom on a three-month bursary from Cambridge University. He soon discovers his elusive boss, Bukowski, is being covertly blackmailed by an estranged wife, and that he himself is to assist the straight-laced Doty on an article about the 'explosion of overt homosexuality' in the city. On an undercover assignment, a secret world is revealed to Raymond: a world in which he need no longer pretend to be something or someone he cannot be; a world in which he meets Joey.

Like so many men of his time and of his kind, Raymond faces a choice between conformity, courage and compartmentalisation. The decision he makes will ricochet destructively through lives and decades until—in another time, another city; in Paris, 2003—Raymond's son Joe finally meets Joey. And the healing begins.

'A sensual, moving story of masks and identities, across two continents and four decades... a strikingly confident debut novel.'
SAMUEL WEST

# Also from Inkandescent

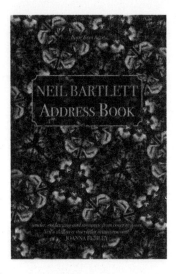

## ADDRESS BOOK
### NEIL BARTLETT

*'Neil Bartlett is a national treasure. I read everything he writes and am always lifted by his skill, humour, political purpose and elegance.'*
DEBORAH LEVY

Address Book is the new work of fiction by the Costa-shortlisted author of Skin Lane. Neil Bartlett's cycle of stories takes us to seven very different times and situations: from a new millennium civil partnership celebration to erotic obsession in a Victorian tenement, from a council-flat bedroom at the height of the AIDS crisis to a doctor's living-room in the midst of the Coronavirus pandemic, they lead us through decades of change to discover hope in the strangest of places.

*"Address Book is completely absorbing; tender, enchanting and a mesmeric read from cover to cover. Neil's skill as a story-teller is unsurpassed. This book is something else. I adored it.'*
JOANNA LUMLEY

# Also from Inkandescent

## MAINSTREAM
edited by Justin David & Nathan Evans

*'A wonderful collection of fascinating stories by unique voices'.*
KATHY BURKE

This collection brings thirty authors in from the mar-gins to occupy centre-page. Queer storytellers. Working class wordsmiths. Chroniclers of colour. Writers whose life experiences give unique perspectives on universal challenges, whose voices must be heard. And read. Emerging writers are being placed alongside these established authors—

Bidisha, Elizabeth Baines, Gaylene Gould, Golnoosh Nour,
Jonathan Kemp, Julia Bell, Keith Jarrett, Kerry Hudson,
Kit de Waal, Juliet Jacques, Neil Bartlett, Neil McKenna,
Padrika Tarrant, Paul McVeigh and Philip Ridley

*'A riveting collection of stories, deftly articulated.*
*Every voice entirely captivating: page to page, tale to tale. These are*
*stories told with real heart from writers*
*emerging from the margins in style.'*
ASHLEY HICKSON-LOVENCE,
author of *The 392* and *Your Show*

# Also from Inkandescent

## THE PALE ONES
### by Bartholomew Bennett

Few books ever become loved. Most linger on undead, their sallow pages labyrinths of old, brittle stories and screeds of forgotten knowledge... And other things, besides: Paper-pale forms that rustle softly through their leaves. Ink-dark shapes swarming in shadow beneath faded type. And an invitation...

Harris delights in collecting the unloved. He wonders if you'd care to donate. A small something for the odd, pale children no-one has seen. An old book, perchance? Neat is sweet; battered is better. Broken spine or torn binding, stained or scarred - ugly doesn't matter. Not a jot. And if you've left a little of yourself between the pages – a receipt or ticket, a mislaid letter, a scrawled note or number – that's just perfect. He might call on you again.

Hangover Square meets Naked Lunch through the lens of a classic M. R. James ghost story. To hell and back again (and again) through Whitby, Scarborough and the Yorkshire Moors. Enjoy your Mobius-trip.

*'A real addition to the literature of the uncanny and an impressive debut for its uncompromising author.'*
RAMSEY CAMPBELL

# Also from Inkandescent

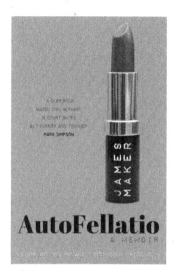

## AutoFellatio

by James Maker

According to Wikipedia, only a few men can actually perform the act of auto-fellatio. We never discover whether James Maker—from rock bands Raymonde and RPLA—is one of them. But certainly, as a story-teller and raconteur, he is one in a million.

From Bermondsey enfant terrible to Valencian grande dame—a journey that variously stops off at Morrissey Confidant, Glam Rock Star, Dominatrix, Actor and Restoration Man—his long and winding tale is a compendium of memorable bons mots woven into a patchwork quilt of heart-warming anecdotes that make you feel like you've hit the wedding-reception jackpot by being unexpectedly seated next the groom's witty homosexual uncle.

More about the music industry than about coming out, this remix is a refreshing reminder that much of what we now think of as post-punk British rock and pop, owes much to the generation of musicians like James. The only criticism here is that – as in life – fellatio ultimately cums to an end.

> *'a glam-rock Naked Civil Servant in court shoes.*
> *But funnier. And tougher'* MARK SIMPSON

Inkandescent Publishing was created in 2016
by Justin David and Nathan Evans to shine a light on
diverse and distinctive voices.

Sign up to our mailing list to stay informed
about future releases:

www.inkandescent.co.uk

*celebrating diversity*

*follow us on Facebook:*

@InkandescentPublishing

*and on Twitter:*

@InkandescentUK